THE *eye* IN THE *thicket*

THE *eye* IN THE
thicket

ESSAYS AT A NATURAL HISTORY

EDITED BY SEÁN VIRGO

thistledown press

Canadian Cataloguing in Publication Data

Main entry under title:
The eye in the thicket

ISBN 1-894345-31-2
1. Natural history—Canada.
I. Virgo, Seán, 1940 –
QH106.E93 2002   508.71   C2002-910323-1

Cover painting: *Golden Days*, 1999, Acrylic in wood,
by Grant McConnell

Cover and book design by Jackie Forrie
Typeset by Thistledown Press Ltd.
Printed and bound in Canada by AGMV Marquis

Thistledown Press Ltd.
633 Main Street
Saskatoon, Saskatchewan
S7H 0J8

Thistledown Press gratefully acknowledges the financial assistance
of the Canada Council for the Arts, the Saskatchewan Arts Board,
and the Government of Canada through the Book Publishing
Industry Development Program for its publishing program.

THE *eye* IN THE
thicket

CONTENTS

INTRODUCTION

SOONER OR LATER the world is revealed through language. More often than not it is later, and we who read are engaging in elegy — for the world as it was, and for the minds which attended to and recorded that world.

The space between world and elegy seems to shrink with each generation. When Thomas Hardy imagined for his memorial "He was a man who noticed such things" he could believe that those things — the "innocent creatures", "the wind-warped upland thorn", the time-distilled voice of his country village — would survive not only himself but those who came after him.

We are, with good reason, less sure about things these days.

The more successful, and troubled, our race becomes the more we understand that "The proper study of mankind" must be the study of that larger family whose troubles reflect our own.

"Natural History" is the most generous name for that study, though it has gone out of fashion: an amateur term, displaced by the compartments of specialized science. The true scientists, though, never lose sight of the context within which they work — they see the connections, their place in "the scheme of things"; they explore, they do not reduce. In the back of their minds, at the forest's heart, in the clearing where Adam/Atom is divided, the fruit of Knowledge must be tasted, philosophically, in the Tree of Life's branching shade.

Natural History involves Nature, of course, but human nature too. The History in it is inseparable from human history.

Two years ago I was asked to compile the first in a series of Essays at a Natural History, a gathering of contemporary voices responding to the contemporary world.

My approach was simple — I solicited work from people whose minds and language I admired and whose experience of the natural world intrigued me. They were also people I could trust not to present themselves, self-annointed, as seers or gurus or prophets. Some were professionals in various fields, others not; but they were all, in my sense of the word, naturalists.

I asked each of them to choose their own subject and to explore it in any way that seemed fruitful to them. They were not to be restricted by any conventional sense of what an "essay" might be.

I allowed myself the same freedom I offered them. *The Eye in the Thicket* is the first in an ongoing series, a cumulative archive. It did not need to be encyclopaedic, or demographically representative. Future volumes, and future editors, will offer further perspectives, further facets of Canadian responses to the world.

I approached twenty-one writers. Inevitably, some would but couldn't; others could but wouldn't. The fifteen essays in this volume have a range of subject matter, styles and tones (the elegiac note may be here but so, praise be, is humour) which delights me. Good writing and loving attention to the world is always a celebration.

I don't want to editorialize on these essays. Individually, and in juxtaposition, they speak for themselves.

I do think that behind almost all of them there is a post-monition, a half-memory, of wilderness, in the true and Balzacian sense of "God without Mankind."

"All landcsapes," Lawrence Durrell claims, "ask the same question: *I am watching you. Are you watching yourself in me?*" Wilderness — for all the space that our country pretends to define itself by — is only a concept: once entered it disappears. It is the greenwood or desert or heart-land, inhabited alike by the wild things, the old gods and races and, at its fringes, by the outlaws and bogeymen. It might have been Eden. We need it, wherever we live, for otherwise we go rootlessly insane (*"When we drove the bear out of the woods he turned up in our minds"*). I believe that we need to sense, in our clearings in time or space, that we are being observed.

The title of this collection reflects that belief. I think now that I borrowed it, unconsciously, from a line in Jan Zwicky's haunting poem, "Recovery" — *"The wren's bright eye in the thicket."* We may have shrunk wilderness to the scope of a thicket, but it does survive — with the potency of snakebite or frostbite, with the shyness of innocent crea-tures, with the seductive textures of wood and water and stone, with the possibility at least that we might step away from "the blood-dimmed tide" of our history and look back in at ourselves.

We shall see.

— *Seán Virgo. Whitemud, 2002*

THE SNAKE-GRASS HILLS

PATRICK LANE

A DRY DENSE HEAT LIES UPON THE HILLS. It gathers in puddles around the flat paws of the prickly-pear cactus. They are lying flat on the crumbling soil, their spines a pale yellow tipped with black. The flesh of the cactus is shrivelled like the skin on the hands of old women. In the cactus palms are the withered shreds of flowers that bloomed and died in the heavy days of spring. Every few hundred yards a pine tree starts out of the earth. The trees are small and grow only a few inches a year. There is no rain in this valley now except for the rare thunderstorm that rises out of the west, battering the dry hills with a sudden flood of water and flame from its lightning. Some of the pine trees have shattered trunks and broken limbs caused by the great storms.

But there is no storm today. There is only the heavy heat: and a sky so thin with blue it is like a whisper above the yellow hills. It is late spring and the boy walks the hills with his brother's .22. His brother doesn't know the boy has taken the rifle. If he did he would kill him. It is his prize possession. The boy wears worn running shoes and patched jeans. He has no shirt and his skin shines like fine deer leather polished into gold. In his pocket are the two boxes of shells he stole from the rifle cabinet at a friend's house. He carries the rifle across his chest like John Wayne does in the movies, the barrel resting back against his arm, the blue metal hot against his skin.

The boy walks these hills like an animal. Every square foot of ground is familiar, every stone, each spare, crooked tree. He knows where the secret places are, the caves above the lake where the black widow spiders hang in the filigree of their webs, the rare desert springs where the animals come to drink, the nests of crows and magpies. And he knows where the rattlesnake dens are in the scree high above the lake. He loves to find them in spring when the snakes move out of their dens deep in the cluttered rock skirts of the hills. Sometimes there are hundreds of snakes. The large ones are as thick as his legs and four feet long. They are the mothers. He doesn't know why he knows this. It is just something he knows. And then there are the little ones, the babies who twine around the bodies of their mothers or cluster in balls. The boy has squatted among them and heard their scales rasp quietly against each other. He has seen their small jaws open and stared at the fangs, those curved blades, hollow-tipped and dangerous.

He has never killed a snake, though others do. There is an old man who walks the hills each year with a forked stick and a machete. The man has killed thousands of snakes. There is a story of a student of this old man who was killed by a snake and that is why the man hunts. The boy has seen the man in the hills and the boy hates him. To the boy the snakes are entirely beautiful. They are spirit creatures born out of the rocks. They are like the magpies. Both creatures are sacred to him The boy thinks that if he saw that old man now he would shoot him and leave him in the hills for the carrion birds, the buzzards, crows and magpies.

These are the boy's hills.

Though others walk them, no one knows them like this boy does. Solitary, alone, he has wandered among their stony outcrops and sat for hours under the thin shade of pines. Today he is hunting gophers; he has killed thirty-two of them. Their tails are in his back pockets. When he returns to town he will sell them for a nickel apiece at the Co-op store where they have three huge jars with a tarantula in each of them, found among the bananas in their crates. He loves them in the way he loves the body-spiders he feeds in the lilac hedges at home. He throws a small grasshopper into each web and then waits for the spider to appear. The killing is always a careful one for the grasshopper knows what comes and his legs are powerful as he rips at the web and tears the thin threads that hold him. But rarely does a grasshopper get away. The spider always wins, testing the grasshopper's struggle with a single outstretched arm. The spider waits until the grasshopper stills, and then moves in with a swiftness that delights the boy. He can see the quick injection of poison and then the rolling of the insect into a narrow case of webbing. If the spider is hungry, he waits for the venom to thin the grasshopper's organs and then he drinks. If not, he retreats to the web's corner where his tunnel is. The grasshopper will be there when the spider's hunger comes.

The boy angles upward through the hills. He knows above him there is a small pond where he can swim among the cries of red-winged blackbirds. He will lie in the water there and watch the swallows skim the surface of the still water as they drink. As the boy crosses over the crest of the last hill he begins to smell something ahead of him. It is a terrible stench. He can taste it in his mouth. Shaking his head he looks around him, but there is nothing he can see except rocks and trees and the thin bundles of bunch-grass growing out of the dust. But there is something some-where. He has never smelled anything like this before.

The smell seems to be coming from his left so he turns that way and begins a slow walk. His nostrils are flared like an animal's. His hair glints in the sun, white against the bronze of his flesh.

Whatever is out there it is ahead of him now. He knows it. And then he climbs a small rise and there it is in a swale among grey stones. The boy hunkers down and rests the .22 against the pale white wood of a fallen pine tree's trunk. He stares at what is just below him. It is huge and it moves as if it were breathing but the boy knows what he sees is not breathing. It is a mountain of maggots. They move in undu-lating waves over the whole body of the dead animal. Under that swollen cloud is a steer. A single horn curves out of the mass. Above the cloud the seething drone of the mothers whines in the air.

What the boy is seeing is death and it is not an ordinary death. It is not the discarded body of a gopher or a squirrel. This is different. He gets up and walks over to the mass of maggots and looks down at them. He has forgotten the smell that is everywhere around him. There are hundreds of thou-sands of the tiny worms. They are eating what is under them, a huge swollen feast the desert has given to them.

Blowfly maggots.

Bluebottle maggots.

Deerfly maggots.

They swarm upon each other as they try to swim down through their sisters and brothers to the rotting flesh below them. A kind of horror moves into the boy. It is as if something has punched him hard in the belly. He turns and picks up a huge stone. He can barely lift it. Trembling, he raises it high above his head and smashes it down upon the swarm. The stone moves through the air and then it hits the mound with a heavy smack and maggots explode around him, small worms flickering against the skin of his chest and arms, spattering his cheeks and lips.

The stone sinks slowly until it disappears.

That is when he begins to run. His hands are everywhere upon him as he brushes the worms off his belly and legs. They are in his hair and he runs his fingers through it, worms slipping among his fingers as he flips them away. He has never known such panic. He is crying now and he doesn't know why he is crying. What he has seen and what he has done is something frightening.

He grabs the rifle as he passes the fallen pine. The worms are gone now, but the smell has returned. It seems to cling to him. It lives inside his nose and mouth. It is as if he has eaten of what was there.

The boy runs through the hills to where the pond is. When he gets there he will throw the rifle aside with the boxes of shells and then he will leap into the warm greasy water and swim under where the cat-tails and snake grass grow. He will stay down as long as he can among the frogs and the leeches. All that will see him will be the birds and one old turtle on a log at the far end of the pond. The turtle will stare at the boy as he thrashes in the water. What he will see is an animal who is moving inside the belly of the pond. Whatever it is, it is full of fear. On the reptile's domed head is the jewelled body of a dragonfly at rest.

What the turtle thinks as he watches, only the turtle knows.

LITTLE BLUESTEM AND
THE GEOGRAPHY OF
FASCINATION

DON GAYTON

IT ONCE WAS A PART OF A GREAT AMBER SEA, this grass. The sea was drained and ploughed long before the invention of the airplane. Hawks and falcons may carry the memory, but no human has ever seen it from the air. But just to imagine looking down on that tallgrass sea, the grassy ocean that stretched from Winnipeg to Texas, and knowing that Schizachyrium was a part, is perhaps enough.

Schizachyrium, it is called. Sky za ky ri um. Skyzakyrium. It is a word so rarely said, you may put the accent on whichever syllable you like. Not sure why it so took me, really. It could have been the strange and haunting name of this prairie icon, this delicate bunchgrass. Or that it is the poster child of a different metabolism, and therefore fascinating by its minority, its ethnicity. Why should it matter, really, that I found it growing quietly hundreds of kilometers outside its range?

Schizachyrium; some assembly required. It is of course a Latin name, but one that takes on meanings of its own. Our nomenclature is based on a dead language because we don't want connotations, we don't want the evolution of meaning, but I wonder. What if the Latin roots of this particular word are so obscure we are forced to invent their meaning? I would have my own legend about the name Schizachyrium, that it doesn't really mean that the seed has a split awn, (*schizein*=to split, *achuron*=chaff) but rather that it refers to the grave and rumpled god Schizachyrio, a lesser light among the Greek deities, one whose particular mojo was Obscure Complexity.

In reality, Schizachyrium is Little Bluestem, a feathery and brick-red grass that once thrived in the lush warm summers of southern Manitoba, and burgeoned southward into Minnesota and on to its limits in Texas. Westward it thins out in Saskatchewan, holding to particular saline seeps at the foot of remnant prairie slopes, in dusty places like Big Beaver or Climax.

To find Schizachyrium all the way out here in southeastern British Columbia, and not only that, to find it on a gravelly and beat-up cutslope above the Bull River, certainly makes one mindful of the obscure complexity of ecology. Schizachyrium has no reason for being on the Bull River. It is a prairie plant, showing progressively less enthusiasm for life the further west it is from its natal Red River Valley, getting sparser and sparser, becoming flat-out rare by the time it reaches the Alberta foothills, and then becoming non-existent, as it gratefully accepts the Rockies as its final barrier. But then voila! reappearing, full of piss and vinegar, on the one gravel cutbank of the lower Bull, and nowhere else.

Now the Bull is one of those mysterious Rockies westslope rivers, a tributary of the Kootenay. To be such a river, it means you started in a range like the Quinn, way up in the fractalled wilderness of the interior Rockies. Then you come boiling down your narrow canyon and burst into the gentle valley at the bottom of the Rocky Mountain

Trench like the Ciccorax released from its dungeon. The Bull always looks to me like it is still surprised that the glacier, which once filled the Trench, is gone. It is as if the river was frozen in mid-step while the glacier was morphed out of the picture, and trees and grass and people were added in.

During those halcyon days at the end of the Ice Age, the Bull carried probably 5,000 gravel pits worth of river rock, sand and gravel down out of the Rockies. Coming into the Trench at right angles, the Bull ran straight into the great stagnated river of ice, so it sluiced and dumped its unceremonious bedload of Rocky Mountain junk right up against the ice flank. As the dwindling glacier halved, and then halved itself again, the Bull had two choices; either cut right through the triangular mountain of gravel it had built, or sneak around the side of it. The Bull of course chose to come right straight down the middle, cutting down through its own rubble. Cut down through it a couple of times, as a matter of fact, as the Bull went from colossal force to the underfit but still vigorous river that it is today.

All this is background of course, to place the rare Schizachyrium on one of those steep cutslopes the Bull carved, and to place it growing on a mixture of Rocky Mountain riverstone and fine gravel.

Well, not just the Bull River, I must confess Eastham spotted it just below the bathhouses at Fairmont Hot Springs in 1939; Brink saw it at the same place in 1950. Milroy reported out from Grasmere in the summer of 1952, saying he encountered it on the "north side of bush road through S.L. 3 of L. 361 K.D. about midway E-W in S.L. 3." I went to S.L. 3, which is near the Elk River, the next major Kootenay tributary south of the Bull. As soon as I got close, I knew the population would be gone. Too many cows, roads, logging shows and alfalfa fields. I tried the old bathhouse site at Fairmont Hot Springs too; the population there fell victim to recreational development. A few more old sightings remain to be checked; the grounds of the Wycliffe Trap and Skeet Club, and the entrance to Kikomun Creek Park. These sites will either provide me with points on a map, or observations on nature and human impact.

There are only a few ways for a prairie plant to get into British Columbia. One way is over the Crowsnest Pass, which means progressively hitchhiking past Fort MacLeod, up the Crowsnest River, down the Elk River and into the Rocky Mountain Trench, deciding at that point to either stay put, as Schizachyrium did, or venture further west through BC's narrow and labyrinthine valleys.

The other way is to tackle the Rockies down in Montana, finding ways west through the Bitterroot and the Clark Fork river valleys and then coasting northward into BC along the Kootenay, the Pend Orielle, or the Columbia.

An equally challenging route is to brave the cold winters of the Peace River country, slipping around the northern end of the Rockies somewhere near Fort Saint John, and then trickling southward along river valleys.

Or, there is the most prosaic route of all, when a Trench rancher buys some prairie hay from Saskatchewan, to get his cows through a late spring. Or a local guide-outfitter picks up a good horse from Manitoba. These things do happen, the pile of manure from the newly arrived animal containing the seeds of a tiny piece of contemporary succession.

There are distribution maps for Schizachyrium. You might think of them as pathetically inadequate records of the various geographical occurrences of the plant, observed and noted by those, like Eastham, Brink and Milroy, who both knew the species by sight and who cared enough to forward their observations. These scattered observations would then be amassed by some aging and reedy botanist, who would turn them into tiny dots on a map. If the taxonomist showed any degree of arrogance, then he or she would draw a sinuous line, connecting the outermost dots, thus creating a distribution map. In drawing the map, the botanist might put a tiny question mark next to a remote and farflung dot, doubting its veracity. Frequently, the distribution map's lines would go no farther than the boundaries of the particular jurisdiction that employed the botanist.

A finished map represents a huge triple jump from the reality of stateless plants rooted in the ground, to an abstracted, incomplete representation along the two dimensions of a political map. Nevertheless I have always loved reading distribution maps, be they of plants, of the northern alligator lizard, or the California bighorn sheep. I could be entertained for hours if I were handed a stack of distribution maps on transparent plastic sheets, all to the same scale. I could shuffle them, and one by one place them over each other, to see if the five-lined skink might have some clandestine geographical relationship with the Kirtland's warbler. Or three-tip sagebrush with the stinkbug, and so on.

With my transparent maps, I could find geographical linkages that might represent evolutionary connectedness, or I could puzzle at the discontinuities where mountain ranges or glaciers or mysterious events have gotten in the way. A Canadian Schizachyrium map would, of course, make no sense at all, with its classic disjunct British

Columbia population. If there was ever a place to put the botanist's accusatory question mark on the map, it would be at Bull River.

Distribution maps could provide more than parlor games, they could become a language. We could communicate via distribution maps. A bilateral distribution, with a boreal population separated from its southern cousins by the Ice Age, could be used to warn of upcoming cold weather, for example. Or the strictly maritime distribution of the Ammophila grass could be a signal that it's time to go to the beach. Communicating this way would be very difficult, and might appear to be like using ancient Mayan to describe semiconductors. To do that would simply be pointless mental gymnastics, and a terrible waste of energy, whereas speaking in a language of species distribution could be embracing the very lexicon of ecosystems. And who knows, the thoughtful shuffling and juxtaposition of those mapped cue cards could generate some startling insights into the soft mechanics of ecology.

Two kinds of people study plants: those who wear lab coats, and those who wear cowboy hats. The former feel most at home in laboratories, the latter are comfortable in the field. Although there is plenty of crossover, these two tribes have a fundamentally different outlook, speak different languages, and each tribe is generally skeptical of the findings of the other. In Canada, long winters force the tribes to mingle somewhat, but even here that division is strong.

The high priests of the lab-coat tribe are the biochemists, the folks who work at the cellular level, and who refuse to look at a plant until it has been through a Waring blender. The lab-coat biochemists periodically generate spectacular advances that the cowboy hats are forced to acknowledge and incorporate, starting right with the explanation of photosynthesis. The body of field knowledge of plants was adjusted to make room for the consequences of that explanation, such as the importance of carbon dioxide, the manufacture of sugars, and the role of respiration. The biochemists generally do not give a damn about the cowboy-hatted ecologists' fascination with how plants *function* in nature. They grow their subjects on styrofoam pellets in climate-controlled phytotrons, only to grind them up and extract their chemicals to see how plants work.

The biochemistry of photosynthesis had long been accepted as a given in plant ecology until the 1960s, when the lab-coat boys dropped another bomb: there was more than one type of photosynthesis. In fact, there were three. They became known by the first products their respective photosynthetic machinery produced — the three-carbon sugar type, the four-carbon sugar type, and the crassulacean acid type. This was precisely the kind of information designed to enrage the cowboys, but it turned out, upon further examination, that these different biochemical groups, at least the first two, fit nicely with one of their pet categories — cool season and warm season grasses. The biochemical machinery of the four-carbon types functioned better at higher temperatures, and these turned out to be all the warm-season grasses, which typically are not active until late June, but grow well through the hot months of July and August, after the cool season grasses have already shut down. The cowboys were able to salvage some dignity by adding a corollary; warm season grasses do well in hot weather, but they also require reliable moisture in late summer, in order to complete flowering and reproduction.

One of those field ecologists was Jan Looman, a reserved and scholarly Dutchman, who probably never wore a cowboy hat in his life. Working first at the Lethbridge and then at the Swift Current Research Station, he was strongly committed to the identification and field observation of native plants. On days when he could not get away from the Research Station, he could usually be found in the herbarium, looking at pressed plants. Looman's primary interest was in plant geography, and the reasons behind why prairie plants were found in some places but not in others. The human species is rarely content with randomness as an explanation, and the urge to understand and classify was particularly strong in Jan Looman, who had a classical European training in ecology. Looman was looking for regional keys to explain plant distribution. Soils could explain some local distribution patterns, but regionally, he concluded that soils were too variable to be a primary driver of distribution. Looman also eliminated altitude as a factor. Even though many classical mountain studies explained plant distribution by changes in elevation, the Canadian prairies are basically a tabletop, with minimal elevation change. And temperature, he concluded, could not be the primary factor either; there were just too many places across the prairies that hit plus 40 degrees centigrade in the summer and then dropped to minus 40 in the winter.

Precipitation was a more obvious driver of prairie plant distribution, Looman hypothesized, as it varied dramatically across the prairies. On a west-to-east axis, precipitation is high in the foothills of the Rockies, decreases rapidly as one moves eastward, hitting a low point somewhere around Swift Current, but then increases slowly towards the Manitoba border and reaches high levels again around

Winnipeg. The south-to-north pattern is similar; OneFour, on the Alberta-Saskatchewan-Montana border, is cactus country, but there is a steady increase in precipitation as you track northward. But Looman knew there was more to the story than just precipitation amount; the seasonal life cycle of a plant had to fit the distribution of precipitation through the growing season. So he began to divide the prairies into zones of distinct spring and summer rainfall patterns, eventually developing eight different areas. Then he painstakingly reviewed the distribution of some 200 typical grassland species, to see if they corresponded to his climatic areas.

The results of Looman's cross-matching were disappointing; all species wilfully crossed and recrossed his climatic boundaries, except for Schizachyrium. The contiguous range of Schizachyrium fit very nicely with a climatic area he called the Moosomin, a narrow belt which stretched parallel to the Manitoba-North Dakota border, and then looped upward into southeastern Saskatchewan. The Moosomin area had medium levels of rainfall in spring, but high levels in the summer. Cool season grasses generally flower in June, but Schizachyrium flowers in August, and adequate moisture during flowering is a necessity for any plant. The result of Dr. Looman's effort was a small, highly qualified, but valuable synthesis of biochemistry, maps, climate and field observation: Schizachyrium prefers areas of adequate spring moisture, abundant summer moisture, and warm summer temperatures.

Looman's hypothesis was a regional one, and made no attempt to explain the localized (known as "disjunct") populations of Schizachyrium, like the one at Bull River. These are left for us to puzzle over.

Schizachyrium shares its uniqueness with another grass known as blue grama, or Bouteloua (boot e loo ah). A tough and curly grass barely a few inches high, it is also a warm season, C4 grass. The seedheads of Bouteloua look like curved caterpillars balancing on the end of a delicate seed-stalk. Bouteloua belongs to another amber sea, but a much harsher, drier one, called the shortgrass prairie. This sea, centered in South Dakota, Colorado and Wyoming, is still partly intact. Unlike tallgrasses like Schizachyrium, Bouteloua and the other members of the shortgrass prairie hunker down to avoid the wind, rather than growing up into it.

There are many different kinds of time, and the one that bedevils plant geographers most is successional time. Schizachyrium might be at Bull River for reasons as mysterious as the galaxies, or as a temporary fluke generated by that prairie hay bale, or as the advance guard of some future invasion of the plant into British Columbia. Or it may be a tattered remnant of some more widespread population in the past. Canada went through a climatic episode six to eight thousand years ago, known as the Hypsithermal, when the climate was warmer than it is today. Isolated populations of Schizachyrium in Ontario and Quebec, as well as the Bull River community, may actually be the remains of a more widespread Hypsithermal tallgrass distribution.

Plants move. The rapid and widespread invasion of Eurasian weeds is testimony to that. But beyond this rapid, human-induced movement of alien species, there is a slower, much slower movement of native grassland species within their own realms. This is the successional time, that we know nothing about. If these plants are in fact moving, why are they moving? Does their movement represent an expansion or a contraction? Are some species moving more rapidly than others?

Sky Zachary Um. That was how one botanist spelled it out for me, when I was still struggling with the pronunciation. My first thought was, this could easily be the name of some first-born child of some New Age couple, rather than the name of the God of Obscure Complexity, or split awn. I am still not sure why the Schizachyrium of Bull River has so taken me, but it continues to multiply in layers of new meaning.

OTHERWISE THAN PLACE

DON MCKAY

I KEEP A RUBBING STONE IN MY POCKET — a piece of glossy basalt from the west coast of Vancouver Island. It's become my palm's companion, always there in moments of stress or boredom, a reassuring weight that's smoother — thanks to the continual wave action which has kept it rubbing against the other rocks on the beach — than skin. Do my fingers, at some level, sense that static energy inside the polish, some residue of the work that went into that gloss, a very local expression of immeasurable force? Its blackness, when I take it out into the light, is darkness with depth, like an eye or a black bear. Sometimes holding it I recall that pebble beach (this is, after all, partly a souvenir) with its huge driftlogs heaped against the forest by Pacific winter storms, its edge of staunch sitka spruce backed by douglas-fir and western red cedar, its gradient of rock from boulder (at the end protected by offshore islets) through gravel to pebble to sand. But mostly it's the outcrop rocks I remember — those raw teeth sieving the sea, constantly breaking the surf into fountains of spray or focusing it into surge channels which can concentrate a wave so that it rushes up in a spout. I had my back turned to what I later realized was a surge channel, one stormy day while I tried to photograph the mosaic of the beach below, and found myself suddenly shoved, camera first, into the rock face: one casual flick from the Pacific which left me drenched.

To think the connection between my introspective black companion and those outcrop rocks taking the brunt of ocean, this requires a stretch of the imagination, including what is perhaps the supreme stretch test — geologic time. I find it a bit easier when I'm back there on the beach in the middle of the forces that accomplished this transformation, but not much. But I think that stretch, and its failure, are further reasons for keeping this smooth eccentric shape in my pocket, contrasting with the locals — those flat metal disks with their two-dimensional portraits of monarchs, moose, beavers and loons.

Now here's a strange thing I have fallen into: when I do get back there (it's been a few years), I'm going to take this rubbing stone and toss it, as casually as I can manage, back among its fellows. I can make this boast because I've done this three times over the last fifteen years or so, selecting another to be my rubbing stone each time the one my fingers have memorized returns to anonymous rock. On the first occasion I was mostly motivated by practical considerations; having spent an hour engrossed by their individual charms, I realized that, were I to indulge myself, I'd risk trouser-drag. But of course, once performed a few times, something ordinary gets to be habit, gets to be practice, gets to be — down the road — ritual gesture. It's no big deal, but I'm wondering, since I'm trying to think the relation between place and wilderness without going dizzy with abstraction, why it feels right. This set of reflections is a set of runs at an answer.

Let me risk a definition. Suppose we try to define place without using the usual humanistic terms — not home and native land, not little house on the prairie, not even the founding principle of our sense of beauty — as a function of wilderness. Try this: "place is wilderness to which history has happened." Or; "place is land to which we have occurred." This would involve asking, for example, not "what's the beach to me?" but "what am I to the beach?" Our occurrence to the land — the act which makes place — could be a major change (homestead, development, resource extraction) or a smaller claim (prospector's stake, survey marker, plastic tape, souvenir stone), but it shifts the relationship; it brings the wild area into the purview of knowledge and makes it — perhaps momentarily, perhaps permanently — a category of mind. "Remember that place we found the huckleberries?"; "Well, I'll tell you where to go if you want to shoot some *real* rapids"; "Now *that's* what I call a nice piece of real estate." Place becomes place by acquiring real imagined borders and suffering removal from anonymity. Sometimes this seems almost wholly benign. But sometimes it is possible to imagine an inner shudder, akin perhaps to that inward quailing you feel when sane authority (the Vice Principal, say, or, for that matter, an author) selects you from out of the safe and faceless crowd in which you swam.

What interests me right now — as you can tell from my opening anecdote and boast — are the possibilities for reverse flow in a relationship that has been so thoroughly one-way. The saga of place has involved colonization, agriculture, exploitation, land use, resourcism and development, sustainable and otherwise. "What we make," Helen Humphreys observes, "doesn't recover from us."[1] I'm not proposing that we can go back, stop farming and living in cities, or undo all the conversions of wilderness to place. But I am suggesting it is good meditative medicine to contemplate otherwise than place as a routine thing. Something like a modification of the practice of fishing from trophy hunting to meat-acquisition to catch-and-release.

How about this? Porches are parts of houses where place can fray out into its other, where it can be acted upon and invaded by pigeons, car exhaust, pollen, noise from the teenagers next door. The porch is the car of the house. Its job is to induce "dwelling", that term in the language of real estate, to work first as a gerund ("dwelling is the art of living along with things"), then as a participle, then as a verb in the active present. It reminds us if we're not too busy firing up the barbecue that place is first a matter of perception, then a set of activities, and only latterly walls and a roof. As John Berger points out, home is represented to the homeless not by a house but by "a practice or set of practices"[2] by which a person creates paths in time and space.

Imagining a counter-current to the steady drag of wilderness into place is, from one perspective, to see a spatial category in temporal terms. Place is where stories happen, where undifferentiated time is given human shape, where infinity becomes history. One of our strongest and most primitive claims on land is probably the grave-site, a piece of property devoted, presumably in perpetuity, to the memory of one person and that person's story; it becomes, literally, a plot. The marble stone on it might well be seen as an address to infinity (or eternity, its religious cousin) on behalf of historical dwelling. The body under it may be rejoining earth, but the name and the plot it comes from will live on as long as marble does. And since we seldom expose ourselves to the bewilderments of geologic time, that looks like forever. Contrary to this may be the gesture of scattering ashes, which implicitly acknowledges process and our participation in it; we join the land in its anonymity. From the vantage point of historical dwelling this goes by the name of oblivion — a name for namelessness, the condition of being unknown or forgotten — a fate to be avoided at all costs.

Perhaps fear of oblivion, of having our names perish with our bodies, goes some way to explaining those extremes of our grip on place which leave the land indelibly marked. In his book *Forests*, Robert Pogue Harrison gives a perceptive account of the opening of the Sumerian Gilgamesh epic. Harrison points out that the hero's motive for wishing to destroy the forest demon is to "Set up his name," which for an ancient Sumerian means hang it stamped in brick. Interestingly, when Gilgamesh approaches the sun god, Utu, with his proposal, Utu responds with a question like the one we asked regarding place as a function of wilderness: " . . . verily thou art, but what art thou to the land?" A durable question, but not one that delays the hero in his willed destruction of the forest and accession to fame.

Harrison also notes that Gilgamesh's urge for an enduring name stems from a particular vision of corpses being floated, as was the custom, down the river. This he relates to Utu as the foundation for his desire to clear-cut.

> "O Utu, I would enter the 'land', be thou my ally
> I would enter the land of the cut-down cedar, be thou my ally."

Utu of heaven answers him:

> " . . . verily thou art, but what art thou to the 'land'?"
> "O Utu, a word I would speak, to thee, to my word thy ear,
> In my city man dies, oppressed is the heart,
> Man perishes, heavy is the heart,
> I peered over the wall,
> Saw the dead bodies . . . floating on the river;
> As for me, I too will be served thus; verily 'tis so.
> Man, the tallest, cannot stretch to heaven,
> Man, the widest, cannot cover the earth.
> Not (yet) have brick and stamp brought forth the fated end,
> I would enter the 'land', I would set up my name."[3]

In Harrison's reading, the cut-down cedars are made to occupy the same space as the human corpses, as they float down the river in the log drive to the city. It isn't greed or the need for building materials that motivates Gilgamesh. Rather, the epic seems to be probing the darkest element in our use of the land — the urge to *lay waste*, to render the material world as *matériel*, to make of our capacity for destruction an enduring sign and so achieve fame. Or, as Harrison puts it:

> There is too often a deliberate rage and venge-
> fulness at work in the assault on nature and its
> species, as if one would project onto the natural
> world the intolerable anxieties of finitude which
> hold humanity hostage to death. There is a kind
> of childish furor that needs to create victims in
> order to exorcise the pathos of victimage within.[4]

Students of the pathology of abuse will probably recognize the shape of this fury as it is expressed in families. And one may also suspect that we are seeing, in this ancient account of heroism, the foundation of the phenomenon known as male rage.

Suppose we take the idea of oblivion and try, as we did with place, to think it from a vantage point outside history. One of its classic statements is Villon's "*Mais ou sont les neiges d'antan*"; suppose we carry this question, which is presumed to be rhetorical, in our heads, or enclosed in a slim volume in your backpack (I'm carrying the lunch, after all), while we walk up the trail up to the Bow Glacier in Banff National Park. We can park at the viewpoint by Bow Lake (although it might be instructive to walk up the river from, say, Cochrane), take photos of ourselves with Mount Balfour in the background, walk around the lake, through the boulder field and across the recessional moraine, up to Bow Falls (spotting a Dipper en route? I hope so) and the foot of the glacier. These *neiges* are truly vintage *d'antan*, dating back to the Wisconsin glaciation, so we have clearly come to the right spot to re-pose Villon's question, which is now obviously not rhetorical, while we munch the trail bars.

But the answers, which could begin with the lake and river we just walked past, proliferate endlessly not only to every-thing downstream (Banff, Calgary, the South Saskatchewan, the great plains, Hudson's Bay) but to that hoped-for Dipper, those Glacier lilies, that boulder field, and everything touched by the water cycle as it expresses itself in the main ranges of the Rockies and eastward. Oblivion, it seems, is teeming.

For another thought experiment with oblivion, we could ask about the whereabouts of the shellfish of yesteryear (*"Mais ou sont les crustacés d'antan?"*) while we walk to my neighbourhood pub. One of the answers to that one might be the sidewalk under our feet, following the long temporal path which begins with an ammanoid in the Devonian and continues through the death of its organism and the deposi-tion of its shell on the ocean floor, the eventual compacting of those fossils into limestone, the elevation of the lime-stone beds through shifts in continents or mountain building, the quarrying of the stone, the mixing of the cement, and finally the pouring of the concrete into this here sidewalk, right here on Fairfield Road. Once we get to the pub we can spend a few minutes sipping our Okanagan Spring lagers and contemplating the busy-ness of oblivion before — grown somewhat dizzy with it — we turn our attention to gossip and the television, on which the Mariners are leading the Indians with two out in the bottom of the eighth.

Otherwise than place, oblivion, geologic time: to contemplate any of these is to countenance our own erasures without rage or despair. I mentioned that I thought such practice good meditative medicine, antidote to our tendency to make places into permanent memorials of ourselves, whether by monumental construction or unforgettable destruction. But I'm under no illusion that we can dwell in that moment or even rest very long in those icy waters, unless we're candidates for some version of sainthood. The possibility of that anti-humanistic extremity is probably best represented by the persona of the mad trapper who walks away from civilization, shedding all its coordinates of identity and place as he goes. I'm thinking in particular of his evocation in Patrick Lane's remarkable long poem *Winter* where the lyric edge speaks directly to that portion of the spirit that craves oblivion, that would walk — or snowshoe — away from name and place and merge with wilderness: a pure anti-type to a hero like Gilgamesh who made the destruction of the forest the making of his name.

> *The man without a name who reversed his snowshoes*
> *and walked forward, head down, shoulders hunched.*
> *The man who climbed the mountains*
> *in the heart of winter, crossing the pass,*
> *heading west into the snow . . .*
>
> *Him walking, head down, shoulders hunched, moving*
> *toward his own quick death, his breath*
> *breaking sharp and hard,*
> *entering,*
> *leaving.*[5]

What's needed is, I think, a small dose of this eros of oblivion, the capacity to think backward or forward from place to its mothering wilderness. That might help impede the tendency to manic ownership and keep the relationship flowing both ways. It might help us see our stories as dissolving into the infinity of details from which they are made. The inscription fades from the marble, and then weeps its minerals into the sea, as surely as the wind will fill those backward snowshoe tracks with snow.

What I miss most about the place I used to live in Lobo Township is the area north of the house we called the meadow — although bush-in-embryo might have been more appropriate, since I'd planted it with white pine, silver maple, cedars and locusts. Probably I miss it because that was the spot where the permeable membrane between place and its otherwise first became apparent to me, where home acquired a frayed edge. I'd beaten a path around its perimeter, one I still walk in memory, passing through the double row of windbreak spruce and along the drainage ditch, through some brambly blackberry canes to the weeping willows in the corner where the ditch right-angled. Beside it was a large granite boulder I fondly hoped was a glacial erratic, and around it some young spruce which screened it from the road — a natural spot to pause, reflect, and even write, sitting on the not very comfortable bench I built there. I know the kids also used it as some form of hideout at various times, but that belongs to their meadows, not mine. Our dog, Luke, also liked this spot — shady, secluded, with good access to the drainage ditch with its muskrats and the meadow with its groundhogs. So, after he got hit by the car, we buried him close by. After that happened, I tended to pause here longer. I will always miss him; but let me tell you, that goddamn dog would chase anything that moved, and he caught a fair number of them. That was the problem — his discipline was totally compromised by his speed and talent. Like everyone's, right? But let's move on . . .

Next there was a line of old poplars where I hung a nesting box for kestrels — one of a dozen or so I put up along the concession roads. It seemed quixotic at the time, more of a gesture of homage to a species I loved than a useful move, until one spring, then another, kestrel families moved in. This gave everything more edge, me included. I spent hours when I should have been marking papers watching the fledged birds learning to fly, an accomplishment which posed for the kestrels some of the problems faced by novice skaters. They were endowed, it seemed, with falcon speed but not with the capacity to stop, so they often overflew the perch, braking too late and tumbling over the far side. (Are all beautiful things, caught at awkward moments, so comical?) Anyway, I was really into kestrels. I met this guy at Hawk Cliff who claimed to have trained one (although you have to wonder who trained whom) to catch pieces of steak he threw up from his barbecue. Sometimes, he said, he'd fake a throw to draw the kestrel's dive, then toss it behind him, the kestrel turning a somersault mid-dive to catch it before it hit the ground. I was hugely envious of this, and briefly considered trying something similar. But what I actually fantasized about was having a kestrel befriend me sufficiently to accompany me to class when I taught "The Windhover" to show those dozy kids how inadequate language — even hyper-extended Hopkinsese — was for those exact and sudden wingbeats.

What am I getting at here? Something like this: each of these stories from the meadow I no longer own (and which has, I'm afraid, moved in the direction of lawn rather than wilderness) gathers place while it also implicitly recognizes its loss: Luke is becoming earth, the kestrels have long since moved on. Perhaps a form of elegy is implied in all story-telling? I don't know; but I do sense that the process can be as much about letting place go as it is about making it, and ourselves, substantial.

On, then, to the locusts — fast growing, beautifully blooming, but very fragile. When an early snow fell one autumn, they caught this unexpected weight in their leaves and bent to the ground. Many snapped. I was busy tending to the damage while Bronwen Wallace was visiting, and of course we were swapping stories. As I recollect, I was standing on a ladder with the chainsaw (bad combination, that) when Bronwen decided to tell the story about the guy whose chainsaw kicked back while he was sawing over his head and embedded itself in his skull. He'd had the presence of mind not to yank it out and unplug the hole, but got himself to Emergency (walking? driving?) with the saw still in his head. True story, so she claimed. Did I finish sawing that locust? Can't recall.

So let me close by risking another pair of definitions: place is the beginning of memory, and memory is the momentary domestication of time. We could continue that walk around the meadow, pausing at the mulberries where the cedar waxwings got drunk, the red maple beloved of orioles, and the grave of the second dog, Sam — and at each the stories would proliferate. But each would come with that temporary, provisional quality built in. Those little walks, whether exercised *in situ* or in memory, exist on the hinge of translation between place and its otherwise, with the flow going both ways, rooting me in place while they simultaneously open — always with that sense of danger, that pre-echo of oblivion — into wilderness.

[1] Helen Humphreys, "Installation," *Anthem*. (Brick Books, London, Ontario, 1999), p. 14.

[2] John Berger, *And our faces, my heart, brief as photos*. (Pantheon, New York, 1984), p. 64.

[3] Robert Pogue Harrison, *Forests*. (U. of Chicago Press, Chicago, 1992), p. 16. Harrison is quoting from Samuel Noah Kramer's translation in his *History Begins at Sumer* (U. of Philadelphia Press, Philadelphia, 1981).

[4] Harrison, p. 18.

[5] Patrick, Lane, "Winter 45," *Winter* (Regina, Coteau Press, 1990), p. 45.

BELOW McINTYRE BLUFF:

NOTES FROM A YEAR

TERRY GLAVIN

WINTER

I. The Chiming of A Clock

IT'S FOUR O'CLOCK IN THE MORNING, and it's snowing. The snow was already starting to cover the whole island yesterday afternoon, and by dinnertime nothing was moving between Miners Bay and Horton Bay Road. With the snow there is also rain and sleet, because the wind is coming from the southwest now. It is coming from out of the Strait of Juan de Fuca, and rolling through Boundary Pass. It is pouring over Heck Hill and Mount Parke and rushing across the tops of the trees.

It's snowing and raining like this everywhere, all across the North Pacific, from Pacheena Point to the Kurile Islands, and beneath the dappled surface of the ocean the great runs of sockeye salmon are swimming through this same night. They came from the Copper River and Bristol Bay, from the Skeena and the Nass, from the Fraser and the Columbia, and now they are a quarter-turn of the planet distant from this coast, and they are moving in their millions, in broad, sweeping arcs, the young in their first winter at sea, and the old in their last.

Among all these, among the old ones, there are some that are already turning, breaking away from the rest. They are different from the others. They are smaller. When they were young, and first reached saltwater at the mouth of the Columbia River, they were among the largest of all the young ones, the size of armour-piercing bullets. But on this night, in their second winter at sea, they are among the smallest of the old ones, and now they are beginning to form their own procession.

Some of them have been far to the south, maybe as distant as the middle of the North Pacific, at the halfway point between San Francisco Bay and Hokkaido's southern capes. But most have spent their time swimming in the cold waters just to the south of the Aleutian Islands, and now, all of them are in the seas between these places, and they are pulling away from all the others to form their own trajectory though the ocean. Among all the old ones, these have the greatest distances to travel, so they are already turning, forming their own distinct orbit. It might have been something in the night sky, or a subtle movement in the needle of some molecular compass, or the chiming of some clock, but they are turning now, leaving the others.

They are leaving the young ones to their pursuit of euphasiids and copepods and amphipods, and they are leaving the other old ones to their chase of small squids and lanternfish, so named because their bioluminescence causes them to appear to the human eye as tiny lanterns carried in strange parades just below the surface, eruptions within a mass movement of forage fish that rises from the mesopelagic depths to the sea surface every night. When the fish rise in that way, it is an event that brings storm petrels and albatross down from the skies. It sets off a mayhem of baleen whales and albacore and neon squid and flying fish. The surface of the sea becomes a roiling mass of rhinoceros auklets and parakeet auklets and shearwaters, and puffins and fulmars and jaegers.

So it is a good place these old ones are leaving, a place of unutterably immense wealth, a place that is rich and lush and alive. But they are leaving anyway, swimming just below the surface, rarely deeper than three fathoms, where the sleet and the snow and the rain mingle with the salt-water.

They are turning now towards the Kurosiwo Current, a swift and purposeful ocean river that arises in the Far Commanders and flows eastward without cease or mercy. It is a relentless thing that has loomed in the nightmares of Asian seafarers from time out of mind. Within sight of Honshu's mountains, great waves rip the rudder away and the winds tear at the shrouds and topple the mast and a few months later there are skulls and splintered timbers on the rocks at Cape Saint James.

Out of the Kurosiwo current came the dead that littered an Aleutian beach in 1782, the bloody footprints that led from the kelp to nowhere, the half-mad ones the Russians found near Sitka in 1805, and the recurring unlucky number, three.

In 1813, the American brigantine *Forrester* found three survivors aboard a Japanese coastal trader, its rudder gone and its masts broken, floating aimlessly 250 sea miles west of Vancouver Island. There had been 35 on board when the junk was swept away in the Kurosiwo eighteen months before. Three years later off Santa Barbara, the *Forrester* found another coastal trader, also with three survivors. They'd lost a shipmate for each of the 17 months that had passed since their ship put out of Osaka. There were fourteen men on a 200-tonne junk bound from Owori to Tokyo in 1833, but it was dismasted and lost its rudder in a gale and the Kurosiwo took it away. A year passed. When the ship washed ashore at Cape Flattery with its survivors, the Makah took them as slaves. There were three of them.

All that starvation and death, and under the ships' keels millions of tonnes of salmon swam, moving in the same eastward-flowing rivers. But the luckless mariners were not fishermen. As often as not they were peasants. They were day-sailors and deckhands indentured in coastal service to carry the tribute of their prefectures to the emperor, a few days' sail away. But they were doomed to Kurosiwo and the Oyashio, the East Kamchatka Current and the North Pacific Current, and it is to these same ghost lanes that the old ones now turn, drawn to their own deaths, and they can do nothing. They will be carried east and then south until they reach the mouth of the Columbia, and they will swim up that river 1,000 kilometres, and then up the Okanagan.

The journey that lies before the Okanagan salmon is far greater than the voyage that awaits the Stuart Lake salmon of the Upper Fraser or the Meziadin salmon of the Nass, and greater even than the salmon from Sakhalin Island and Kamchatka with which they have been spending these past months, the salmon that have haunted the imaginations of the Kamchadals, the Koryaks, the Nivkh, and the Ul'chi peoples, from time out of mind. The sockeye now heading eastward along the ghost lanes leading back to the North American coast have come farther than even the salmon from the Kvachina, the Bolshaya, the Onlukovena and the

Amur, on China's northern frontiers. And now they are bound for their home gravel in the Okanagan River, where they will spawn and die in the mesquite and the bunchgrass country downriver from McIntyre Bluff, which is a place as haunted as the rest.

As the story goes, a group of marauders from the north, young men from the Secwepemc country, were making their way across a high sage plateau on a moonless night in late summer. An old blind man warned them that the plateau ended in a sheer drop into a deep canyon but they didn't listen, and over they went, one by one. Their blood stained the cliff face below McIntyre Bluff and their flesh was strewn in the branches of the silver willows. In the morning some local Inkameep women were making their way along the river, and they thought some deer must have fallen from the cliff. Then they saw the crumpled bodies of the young men among the saskatoon bushes, and they turned their faces away.

But that was in the summer, and now it is winter. It's four o'clock in the morning, and it's snowing.

II. *Rounding the Alaskan Gyre*

It's still snowing. It has been a week. It is ridiculous, and I am crawling on my belly through some of the darker and more wretched places underneath my house, armed with a propane torch. The pipes are frozen somewhere between the well shed and the faucets in the house and there's no cure for it but to slither through the dark, through the muddy detritus of rusted paint cans, skeletal remains, murder weapons and bits of old furniture. The point is to find exposed sections of pipe, aim the propane torch, and pray that the house doesn't go up in flames.

Soon, the Okanagan sockeye will be skirting the defiles of the coastal downwelling domain to find their way south out of the North Pacific Current to the California current. By now, they are leaving the ocean haunts of a race of dwarf cherry salmon from the Amur River, and the haunts of the Primorye's sea-run taimen, a fish just like a steelhead but as big as a grown man, a still-existing relic of the ancestor of all salmon, the oldest salmonid known to evolutionary biology. And as the Okanagan sockeye are making their way around the southern orbit of the Alaskan gyre, I am underneath my house with a propane torch and the island is sullen and silent but for the dripping snow, the same kind of heavy and wet and dreary snow that drove Stephen Krasheninnikov near to madness in 1736, during his first winter with the Kamchadal people of Kamchatka, on the far side of the ocean.

It was from the Coast Salish people of the island where I live that sockeye got their name, from "sukkai". But it was Krasheninnikov who introduced sockeye to western science as "narka", the name the Kamchadals gave their beloved red salmon, and that is how it came to pass that Linnaean taxonomy classifies the creature as Oncorhynchus nerka. Krasheninnikov was 24 years old that first winter in Kamchatka. He'd been sent there because the Empress Anna wanted a full accounting of her eastern possessions, and the Russian Academy of Sciences had assigned Krasheninnikov to the task with a small company of cossacks to assist him. It rained and it snowed, then the snow fell and it rained again, and the Kamchadals relieved the boredom with hallucinogenic mushrooms. A cossack tried some, remarked that he was inclined to take a nice, brisk walk, and he kept walking until he died.

Among the phenomena Krasheninnikov observed that winter was an abundance of giant rats, and he insisted that the Kamchadals revered them, and I was pondering this at a dank and vile junction underneath the house when I heard something moving. I turned to look, and I saw some kind of animal, with mottled, wet fur, groaning and slithering through the dark.

The story about the last cougar on this island involves the barking of dogs echoing against Heck Hill and Flag Hill in the late 1940s as the cougar is chased from Horton Bay right across to Dinner Bay, where the farmers catch up to it. They shoot it, and the kids are let out from school to go and have a look-see. There had been war between us and the raccoons for our chickens, which the raccoons won. So the thing under the house was certainly not a cougar, but bigger than a raccoon, and when my head shot up among the cobwebs and the top of my skull bounced off a support beam, I found myself surrounded by monsters.

On this very island, it would have been commonplace only a century before to hear rumours of tree-strikers, peculiar little men possessed of the habit of knocking down trees for no apparent reason. They were said to move about somehow on one leg, with a claw in it. Perfectly reasonable people attested to such things. There is an odd digression in his "History of Kamchatka", first published in Saint Petersburg in 1754, which refers to a "sea monkey" the naturalist George Steller claims to have seen off the Alaskan coast in the 1740s, in the same waters the Okanagan sockeye would be traversing by now. This beast was described as having a head like a dog, large eyes, and a beard. Krasheninnikov said the sea monkey could "stand erect like a man" above the waves, and would play "a thousand apish tricks" alongside ships.

Then there's the Cadborosaurus, a sea-serpent which has been the subject of numerous sightings around Victoria and the Gulf Islands for most of the 20th century. The most convincing story came from the reputable west-coast writer and former whaler William Hagelund, who captured what he believed was a baby cadborosaurus at Pirate's Cove at De Courcy Island, just off Galiano Island, in 1968. Hagelund described the creature as having sharp, small teeth, with plate-like scales down its back, a pair of small, flipper-like "feet" and two tiny flipper-like fins. It was about the size of a cat, and Hagelund and his son put the thing into a bucket on the deck of the family's sloop. Their intent was to bring it to the Pacific Biological Station in Nanaimo, but the animal thrashed around in its bucket all through the night, and Hagelund took pity on it. Concerned it would die, Hagelund lowered the bucket over the side and let the thing go.

I've always thought that the creature Hagelund encountered was a fish known as a deep sea daggertooth, *Anatopterus pharao*, which ranges from Japan as far north as the Bering Sea and as far south as the California Coast. It is hideous and preposterous, for all appearances like artists' renderings of cadborosauri, and while it usually swims at great depths, it has been encountered in three fathoms.

When I came to my senses the tongue licking my face belonged to Shadow, my German Shepherd. But the whole thing had been enough, and I crawled out into what little daylight the winter sky allowed. We ran a long hose from the neighbour's place for three days.

SPRING

I. Killing the Wolf

The wolf was killed this morning. A posse of ill-equipped farmers hunted it down and killed it on Samuel Island, which lies between Saturna Island and Mayne Island, where I live. It was shot by Samuel's Mike Graham.

Since last September, it had been swimming from island to island, attacking and killing animals. On Mayne, it killed several sheep from Punch Robson's place down on Horton Bay Road. On Saturna, it killed several feral goats, a week-ender's golden retriever, about a dozen of the Campbells' sheep down near Saturna Beach, and a llama from Breezy Bay Farm, which it killed on Mount Fisher. It almost killed Minnie, Priscilla Ewbank's pony, only Priscilla scared the thing away.

It was a Vancouver Island wolf, a southerly remnant of the upcoast salmon wolves, unique among the planet's wild dogs for being dependent on salmon for protein, in the same strange way that coastal black bears and grizzlies would vanish without salmon. Creatures that rely upon salmon in this way include weasels, coyotes, seals, otters, red fox, shrews, mice, squirrels, hawks, ravens, crows, gulls, king-fishers, jays, wrens, and dippers. Analysis of grizzly bear bones in the shadow of the Rockies, more than 1,000 kilo-metres from the sea, show that as much as 90 per cent of the carbon and nitrogen in the bears' diets came from

salmon. Half the bald eagles of the North American continent, some from as far away as Wyoming, Saskatchewan
and Arizona, routinely congregate in large concentrations
during the chum spawning season on British Columbia's
salmon rivers.

From Johnstone Straits to Gribble Inlet, killer whales
hunt the inlets and the channels for seals and sea lions,
but also for black-tailed deer. The deer swim from shore to
shore, and a phalanx of black fins approaches. One of the
fins moves out ahead of the rest, in the direction of the deer,
then the fin disappears. A moment later, the deer disappears beneath the waves.

It is almost certain that the wolf the farmers killed on
Samuel Island this morning came to our islands by swimming from Vancouver Island, across Sansum Narrows to
Saltspring, say, where it dog-paddled across the channels,
possibly to Prevost, and then to Mayne, Lizard, and
Saturna. But the killer whales that roam the waters around
these islands are resident Straits orcas, and there are none
like them anywhere. They are matrilineal salmon-eaters.
They do not care for seals or sea lions or coastal deer or
wolves, and so the wolf Mike Graham shot had been free
to swim from island to island the way it did. Its tracks were
seen on islands as far off as Cabbage and Tumbo. It appears
to have made a lair for itself on Saturna, somewhere up on
Mount Warburton Pike.

II. The Collision of Biologies

The sound was bloodcurdling. It came from deep within
the cedar trees. It was a moonless night, without wind, and
at first I thought I was hearing a cat being tortured, or an

old woman screaming in pain. It was more than creepy let me tell you.

There is nothing pretty about the sound of a peacock. Not when it caterwauls before it goes to sleep. Not at dawn, either. Its morning repertoire begins with what a gigantic kazoo might sound like, and it carries on with a wailing and plaintive *help, help, help,* and the sun isn't even up and all you can think about is how righteous and proper it would be to serve the creature with the fiery consequence of a 12-gauge Franchi pump-action PA3/470 riot shotgun with 1,145 feet-per-second muzzle velocity (standard barrel).

How it came to pass that a huge peacock arrived in the trees behind my place in the middle of this island and then set about a daily routine of intimidating the bantam chickens and the cats, Marlow and MJ, and Diesel, the German Shepherd next door, is uncertain. There are several stories. My neighbours, Dan Hafting and Katja Korinth, who have suffered the most, concluded that the following story is the most plausible.

For as long as anyone around here can remember there has been a muster of feral peafowl on nearby Curlew Island, which is also home to a small herd of Himalayan ibex, while we're on the subject. Other creatures have been spotted on Curlew from time to time, leaving an eerie Island-of-Doctor-Moreau feeling about the place, especially when you're rowing down Lizard Channel and a bone-chilling scream comes from the island's interior and out of the corner of your eye a head with horns of some kind, I swear to God, disappears behind a gnarled arbutus.

Somebody from Saltspring Island got fed up with his pet peafowl. He heard about Curlew, and decided to abandon them there, but Curlew's feral peafowl didn't welcome the new arrivals. Shunned by their gone-to-seed relatives, the abandoned pets flew the short distance to Potato Point, here on Mayne, sometime this past winter.

That's the story.

All I know is that these days, there is a peacock that wakes me up after I fall asleep at night, and wakes me up again before sunrise, every morning, and all I can think of is how useful it would be to have on hand one of those new carbon-steel nine-millimetre Para-Ordnance 14-5 light-weight double-action pistols everybody's talking about.

To be honest, a peacock is a beautiful thing. It's throat is a shimmering neon turquoise, its tail fan is like a bouquet of brilliant flowers on bright green stems.

But there is nothing pretty in what has become of Sidney Island, which lies a couple of hours by boat to the south of us. The once-lush undergrowth is gone. In places it's like a parched savannah with bark stripped off the trees after the wildebeests have been through. The damage has been done by fallow deer that would-be venison farmers brought from Europe years ago. Sidney Island is a narrow sliver of a thing, perhaps three kilometres in length. There have been times when the island's fallow deer population has numbered 3,000 animals. Fallow deer are not at all like west-coast deer. They graze, like goats. They chew everything that grows, down to the root. They are vermin. Nothing will help the situation this side of platoons of islanders equipped with ITT Nightquest Gen-3 night-vision goggles and breech-loading M203 40-millimetre single-shot grenade launchers as well as Colt AR15 9-millimetre assault rifles with ribbed "shorty" handguards, bayonet lugs and flash suppressors.

But then there is the ubiquitous broom, the green weed that produces what some weekenders consider to be lovely yellow island flowers every spring. Like fallow deer, broom came from Europe. It arrived on this coast in 1850 with Walter Colquhoun Grant, who got some seeds from the British consul in Hawaii with a view to planting some on his farm at Sooke. He did, and now broom is doing what fallow deer do, only everywhere — all over Vancouver Island, the Gulf Islands, and the Lower Mainland. It chokes the life out of local plants and shrubs. It acidifies the soil and crowds out everything else. It is not pretty. Eradicating it is near to impossible. Just controlling it involves root-pulling and backbreaking labour, and it is at this point that we must acknowledge that despite the beauty of our weapons, the islands where I live are under assault from forms of life so cunning and resilient that conventional artillery is useless against them.

There are armies of European black slugs engaged in nighttime battles with the Gulf Islands' famous *Ariolimax columbianus*, the giant banana slug, and the locals are losing. Bullfrogs from the U.S. deep south have established themselves on Southern Vancouver Island, and they're chasing out colonies of Pacific tree frogs, rendering spring evenings silent of the tree frog's chorus.

Japanese sargassum weed is a seaweed that arrived in the Strait of Georgia several years ago and is now crowding out local seaweed species. Sargassum is believed to have arrived in the ballast of a freighter, and from here it moved on to Europe, where it arrived with a shipment of British Columbia oysters that shellfish farmers had hoped to establish on the coast of France. Even the B.C. oysters weren't native. Like sargassum, our oysters came from Japan. We have a native oyster, but it is a flat, pancake-like mollusc that's not of much use to anyone. The delicious oysters that we pry from the rocks and eat raw at low tide down at Edith Point and Georgina Point are the descendants of Japanese oysters that were first seeded on the far side of the Gulf at Boundary Bay in the 1890s. Now they're everywhere, and to be honest, I can't think of a bad thing to say about interloping oysters.

In the same way, I can't think of a bad thing to say about crested mynahs. Among North Americans, only Vancouverites and Victorians will be in any way familiar with these birds. But the last time mynahs were a common bird in these cities and their environs was the 1970s. Unlike so many endangered songbirds that are indigenous to the West Coast, crested mynahs arrived here only in the 1800s, with Chinese immigrants, who brought the birds as pets in cages. Eventually, enough birds were freed or escaped that they established a local flock, and over the years, their numbers grew.

Crested mynahs will gladly mimic people, and they'll mimic other birds and any number of the sounds of the city, like sirens and car alarms. They used to gather in small flocks on the sidewalks, casually poking around for bugs. Think of a gathering of old men, each with his arms folded behind his back, each deep in thought, each walking in a circle, now and then skipping a step, hopping on one foot. Their feathers are jet black, their beaks bright yellow and they've got a little nob on their foreheads. Only when they fly away can you see the distinctive bright white round patch on each wing.

The mynahs are still seen occasionally, but they have become as rare as kingbirds, winter wrens and nuthatches. The reasons are many. Cats, for one. And pavement, where the trees and the fields used to be, and pesticides and herbicides, and not least, another 19th-century arrival, the European starling. Ever since a certain Eugene Schieffelin got the bright idea in 1890 that New Yorkers would like William Shakespeare's writings more if the city was alive with the birds mentioned in Shakespeare's works, starlings have ravaged North America's indigenous songbird populations. Starlings are prolific breeders, they beat up on smaller birds, steal their nests and eat their eggs. Like Sidney Island fallow deer, they are vermin, and they are bullies, and in this way they are like European green crabs, recent arrivals that devour massive quantities of juvenile oysters and clams, as well as juvenile Dungeness and red rock crabs.

Green crabs were first sighted in Barkley Sound in the late 1990s. They've since been found in Clayoquot Sound and in Esquimalt Harbour. Then there's the tens of thousands of Atlantic salmon that have escaped from fish farms to take up residence in local waters. The presence of these disease-prone, genetically-manipulated creatures in the Pacific is setting the stage for what University of Toronto evolutionary biologist Mart Gross calls a "classic collision of biologies" with its wild Pacific cousins. The way such collisions usually play out, the locals lose.

It is war.

Whether or not peafowl are engaged in this kind of warfare depends on how much sleep you've been getting lately. It depends on how you look at these things. It depends on what you believe. Medieval Christians believed that angels' wings were made of peacock feathers. Javanese Muslims say a peacock guards the gates of paradise. There is an old Chinese story that peacocks can make women pregnant just by looking at them. In an old Hindu tradition, a peacock looks like an angel, walks like a thief, but has the voice of the devil himself.

SUMMER

I. Return of the Bats

The cruise ship *Galaxy* entered Vancouver harbour yesterday morning, and unbeknownst to the ship's captain, a dead fin whale, close to 20 metres in length and weighing probably 50 tonnes, was more or less impaled on the ship's bow. It was on the television news. It was fascinating, in the way that traffic accidents are fascinating, and last night, a bat flew into my bedroom, and I panicked because I thought it was a giant moth.

Something must have happened when I was a baby. I recoil in horror from moths, and the bat flapping around above my bed was behaving just like a giant black moth, and I confess that at the moment this was happening I comprehended it as something dangerous, even evil. But it was a bat, and bats appear in the night skies at about the same time that the year's returning sockeye first approach the North American coast. The runs bound for all the rivers south of the Bering Sea appear tentatively at the remotest places, like Duu Guusd, where Juan Perez emerged from a fog bank in 1774 to find himself surrounded by a flotilla of Haida in oceangoing canoes.

Nobody knows for certain where the bats spend their winters. It has only been a few years since the first time anyone saw a bat in British Columbia in winter. That was the discovery of a cave in the mountains above Tahsis, the inlet on Vancouver Island where Maquinna's dancers mimicked Europeans, Hawaiians and Chinese in a performance for George Vancouver in 1792. There were several species of bats there. They were sleeping, and it is not known what sort of Kurosiwo current might be found in the early summer skies, and it is not known which direction that current comes from. Some side streams appear to arise in the south, and they bring little brown bats by the hundreds of thousands to the burnt sage country east of Kamloops, where the young men who died at McIntyre Bluff came from.

I once climbed into the attic of an abandoned Catholic church in that country, in the Secwepemc village of Squilax, to know what it would be like to be swarmed by 3,000 pregnant female little brown bats. The church, which has since burned down, had been abandoned long before because one day the ceiling collapsed under the accumulated weight of several years of bat guano. The female bats had colonized the attic and put it to use as a nursery, and there were stalactites of crystallized bat urine hanging from the ceiling and metre-deep piles of bat guano on what was left of the rafters, and it was muggy and warm and alive with the sound of the bats hissing and defecating.

The bat in my bedroom was probably one of the myotis bats, perhaps a Yuma, which would fit in the palm of my hand. I am happy that a bat this size can eat 600 mosquitoes an hour. I am content in the knowledge that without bats, agave plants would not be pollinated and I would never have known what it is like to be falling-down drunk on tequila, and that bats are not flying rats, or flying mice, but are actually quite closely related to primates, and that the world's smallest mammal is Thailand's famous bumblebee bat, which weighs less than a penny.

But the problem with bats is that they are not glamorous, which is why everybody knows about the Vancouver Island marmot and the marbled murrelet but hardly anybody knows about Keen's long-eared bat, which is facing the same kind of fate. It is worse for fish. Of the 85 types of fish known to occur in British Columbia, 34 are vulnerable, threatened or endangered. Some have been pushed off extinction's cliff edge. In 1956, the B.C. government poisoned the Dragon Lake whitefish into oblivion to make way for a stock of rainbow trout. A few years ago, somebody released catfish into Hadley Lake on Lasqueti Island, and two species of sticklebacks vanished. It is hard to get any attention if you're an Enos Lake benthic stickleback or a Missezula Lake chiselmouth or a Cultus Lake sculpin or a Tyhee Lake giant pygmy whitefish or an Umatilla dace.

On Sumas Mountain, about 50 kilometres east of Vancouver, there exists a mysterious animal that shares the same endangered-species classification as the spotted owl, but lacks even the demi-celebrity of the Pacific giant salamander. It is a 40-million-year-old haplodon, a relic of the Upper Eocene, the sole mammalian occupant of an evolutionary cul-de-sac that was teeming in the days when woolly camels and sloths once roamed North America. It doesn't help that the creature spends most of its life in underground tunnels and comes out almost exclusively at night. It rarely strays more than 200 metres from its home burrow during its entire life.

Its scientific name is *Aplodonta rufa*. While the first hint of its existence was whispered to western science in the 1806 journals of Merewether Lewis and William Clark, scientists have shed little light on its habits. The academic literature remains informed as much by folklore as by clinical, methodical observation. In the standard reference texts, the animal is said to weep great tears when distressed, grind its teeth when angry, and, by some unknown means, utter loud booming sounds.

Lewis and Clark made note of an animal which the Lower Columbia people favoured "in forming their robes, which they dress with the fur on them and attach together with sinews of the Elk or deer," and which they called the "siwelel." It has gone by many names: Ground bear, whistler, mountain boomer, kickwilly, showtl, ogwoolal, oukala, kula possum, giant mole, ground beaver, and kulata.

Among the very few people who have even heard of the thing, it is most commonly called the mountain beaver, although it isn't anything like a beaver. At a distance it could be mistaken for a beaver without a tail, maybe, or a muskrat, but there are few people who have ever seen one, even at a distance. The Sumas Mountain haplodon is the coastal subspecies *Aplodonta rufa rufa*, which ranges well into Washington state but is confined in Canada to Sumas Mountain and the mountains south of the Fraser Valley from about Cultus Lake to, say, Hedley. There is another Canadian subspecies, *Aplodonta rufa rainieri*, that can be found from around Princeton to Merritt. There's very little difference between the two — a slightly more reddish hue to the coastal species' fur, for instance. There are two other subspecies north of the Columbia River, and four subspecies south of the Columbia, which persist in tiny pockets in California. And that's all there is.

In his Yellowstone diaries, the great American naturalist John Muir wrote that mountain beavers routinely alter the flow of streams and construct canals to feed intricate subterranean watercourses and to keep the shrubs it likes well-irrigated. "It is startling," he wrote, "when one is camped on the edge of a sloping meadow near the homes of these industrious mountaineers, to be awakened in the still night by the sound of water rushing and gurgling under one's head in a newly formed canal."

Could be. We just don't know much about these beasts, and we never knew much about the creature that came to be called the giant sea mink, an amphibious Atlantic-coast mammal of some kind that Sir Humphrey Gilbert described in the 16th century as "a fyshe like a greyhound." Two centuries later, the English naturalist Joseph Banks described the animal as most closely resembling an Italian greyhound, "legs long, tail long and tapering. . . it came up from the sea." Environment Canada uses the term sea mink to describe an extinct animal about which little is known beyond those early descriptions, and from a few bones found in aboriginal kitchen middens in present-day Maine.

II. Cities at the Bottom of the Sea

The old ones have passed Duu Guusd now. Other sockeye are beginning to make their way home to the Nass and the Skeena, where Raven made the way for them somewhere near the beginning of time. There are sockeye turning now for their long voyage home to the Somass River on

Vancouver Island's west coast, and to the Fraser River, where X:als, the great transformer, first placed them. But the old ones bound for the Okanagan are already making their way down the outer coast, and there will be sportsmen and trollers and seiners and gillnetters for much of the way, and it will be Coyote who welcomes them, not Raven and not X:als.

And I can't pick up a newspaper without reading about another outrage committed by Coyote on the poor people of Vancouver. Babies nearly snatched from their carriages. Schoolgirls chased across soccer fields, toddlers robbed of their ice cream cones at Jericho Beach, a Coquitlam kid bitten and the B.C. Wildlife Federation proposing a coyote hunt through the backstreets. At a Vancouver city council meeting, a councillor declares that the shooting must begin soon, because coyotes have become as great a threat to urban life as a plague of cougars or bears.

The environment ministry urges calm. Yes, there have been 1,017 complaints about coyotes throughout Greater Vancouver and the outlying suburbs in the past year. But the majority of complaints were really just sightings, or attacks on farm animals in the valley, or suspected attacks on pets. Attacks on humans: Three.

Over the same period, just within Vancouver's city limits, there were 2,287 complaints about regular dogs, the kind people keep as pets. Attacks on humans: 250. But it doesn't matter. We must kill coyote, they say.

In the days following the Great Flood, there was a great witch who menaced the mouth of the Columbia River, and it was Coyote who fought with her and subdued her and tied her to a board and put her out to sea, throwing open the river to allow the sockeye to pass upstream. It was

Coyote who took a great knife to slay the monster at Celilo Falls and commanded the seagulls to escort the sockeye further upriver, to all the places where the people lived, and there he taught the people how to catch them, with dipnets. And now it is to the Columbia that the old ones race through the sea, and they have become like flocks of birds flying over other cities, cities as big as Vancouver, built from hexactinellid sponge reefs, ghost-like animals that have been growing from the skeletons of their dead kin for the past 9,000 years at the bottom of Queen Charlotte Sound and Hecate Strait.

Above the towers of these cities the old ones now swim, traversing the largest biotic structures on the planet, each a metropolis of thousands of mound-like eruptions, some seven storeys high, all connected in a dead and living mass of the same species. The cities are several kilometres in width, and they are teeming with sea life. They were thought to have gone extinct 145 million years ago, leaving their ruins only in the great fossil outcrops of Germany, Romania, Portugal, and the Caucasus Mountains. They were discovered by Kim Conway and Vaughan Barrie of the Geological Survey of Canada's Pacific Geoscience Centre. But they have been known to the old ones from the days that followed the Great Flood, when Coyote called them home.

AUTUMN

It is a windy October afternoon. There are brilliant red sumac bushes along the banks of the Okanagan River, which follows a course below McIntyre Bluff no wider than a city street. There is a dam here, operated by the South

Okanagan Land and Irrigation District. It is situated directly below McIntyre Bluff, which is just north of the Deer Park Estates trailer park and Gallagher Lake Autobody, on Highway 97. It is a small dam, but it is enough to form a barrier the old ones can't pass.

The McIntyre dam began as a weir to divert water into a ditch to irrigate orchards of the bright red Okanagan apples that made a way of life for soldiers returned from the First World War. In the river just below the dam on this overcast afternoon there is another bright red thing, a sliver of scarlet, blood red. It is a solitary buck sockeye, one of the old ones. It is straining against the current below the dam's sluicegates. It is near death, but it wants to keep going upstream, on through Vaseaux Lake and beyond Okanagan Falls, where Okanagan and Spallumcheen and Similkameen peoples once crowded the banks with their dipnets. It wants to continue on as its ancestors did, through Skaha Lake, which comes from the Okanagan word for dog, from dog salmon, the chum salmon. It wants to continue up the winding river as its ancestors did, and as the chinook salmon as big as young boys once did, into Okanagan Lake.

But it cannot pass McIntyre Dam, and so it lingers there, alone, beneath the bluff that was once stained red with the blood of young men, as red as its own body has now become, as red as the apples that grow from the hills all around. But soon it must float back downstream to find a mate among the others that have survived to return to the South Okanagan's dry and rocky hill country.

A ten-year-old kid could design a fish ladder at McIntyre. It would cost about the same as a culvert. The rudimentary material required to blow up the dam would cost even less. The same thing can be said about the dams farther upstream, at Okanagan Falls and at Penticton, but that country is the heartland of the old Social Credit kingdom and a new aquatic ecosystem has been built there, involving legions of introduced species. There are small-mouthed bass and large-mouthed bass, and brook trout and carp and crappie. They are not like broom or sargussum weed or starlings. They are easy to kill. But there also new suburbs that span the broad valley's horizons. There are fundamentalist Christian churches and jet-ski races and dirt-bike tournaments and entire subdivisions filled with retired Alberta businessmen.

The sockeye that have come home to the Okanagan are about 25,000 in number, but even in this decimated state they form the most robust of the three sockeye populations that remain in the entire Columbia River basin, a landmass half the size of Europe. Several hundred kilometres downstream, the Wenatchee sockeye have also arrived home, and there are about 6,000 of them that have survived this year's journey. Across the mountains to the southeast, far up the Snake River at Redfish Lake in Idaho, the Columbia's third tribe of sockeye, a relic, has also arrived after a 1,500-kilometre journey from saltwater. There are 400 of them this year. The year before, there were only 35. But the year before that, there were only three.

Apart from those few Redfish Lake salmon, the Okanagan sockeye have travelled farther in freshwater than any other race of sockeye in the Pacific, and unlike any other sockeye in the Pacific, they almost always return as three-year-olds. Most sockeye return from the sea as four-year-olds, or five-year-olds. But not these. They are different, and they are intrepid and ferocious.

Throughout the summer they fought their way through an ocean gauntlet of fishboats arrayed against them in Southeast Alaska, and in the waters all along the British Columbia coast, and there were more at the mouth of the Columbia River at the Washington-Oregon border.

They entered the Columbia River before the end of June. They struggled through a series of tribal fisheries along the banks of the Columbia, and then they fought their way around nine mainstem dams — the Bonneville, the Dalles, John Day, McNary, Priest Rapids, Wanapum, Rock Island, Rocky Reach, and Wells. They'd made it past Wells by mid-July.

At the confluence of the Columbia and the Okanagan, they lingered. For weeks, they swam up and down the Columbia, waiting for the summer to wane and the water pouring out of the Okanagan to cool. Some of them ventured as far upstream as the great Chief Joseph Dam, but they had returned to the Okanagan mouth by mid-August, and up the Okanagan they went.

By September, they had made their way into Osoyoos Lake, on the Canada-U.S. border. The countryside to which they had returned was forbidding and unwelcoming. It is a place where one third of all British Columbia's endangered animal species can be found, and one third of all B.C.'s endangered plant species, too. It is a singularly peculiar landscape, with eight species of invertebrates found nowhere else in the world and 28 species of invertebrates found nowhere else in Canada.

This is not the sort of countryside where salmon are known to flourish. It has nothing to do with the temperate rainforest, which regulates salmon spawning habitat with elaborate arboreal mechanisms that control hydrology, gravel distribution, temperature and nutrients. There are no cold mountain streams here. Instead, there is prickly pear and sage and tiger salamanders. There are sage thrashers, night snakes and screech owls. There are rubber boas, spotted bats, painted turtles and Great Basin spadefoot toads. It is a hardscrabble northern territory of the Sonoran desert, and it is becoming more inhospitable to salmon as the years pass.

When they were making their way around the Wells Dam, and even after they had crossed the border into Canada at Osoyoos Lake, there were still 50,000 of them left. But the countryside was still shimmering in the heat. The south end of Osoyoos Lake was dead water, the central basin of the lake was little better, and below Anarchist Mountain there was only a treacherously narrow band of water left for them to navigate. Above it, the water was too hot for them to survive. Below it, there wasn't enough oxygen to breathe. So they had to pass between these two deaths. Half of them died in the lake.

Those that survived are spawning now. All that remains for them is a five-kilometre stretch of the river between the town of Oliver and the McIntyre Dam. Most of them are spawning in a single kilometre of the river just below Park Rill Creek, within the Osoyoos Indian reserve. It is the last wild reach of the Okanagan, the only place where the river hasn't been turned into a canal. In the clear and cool river, they are spawning in their thousands, their bright red bodies undulating against the gravel, and it is unspeakably beautiful.

As the story goes, in the days following the Great Flood, they were brought to this very reach of the river by Coyote himself.

He carried them here on his tail.

HOW DO WE KNOW
BEAUTY WHEN WE SEE IT:
TWENTY MEDITATIONS
ON STONES

SUSAN MUSGRAVE

1. Touchstones

I have never worn precious stones — diamonds in my earlobes, square-cut emeralds on my fingers or sapphires blue as the unappeasable sky. For me, jewels, in their flashiness, are places lonelier than darkness. A beach pebble unadorned, a river rock licked into an egg — the wild, tumbling-free stones — are the ones most precious to me. Stones pulled by tides, polished by the moon; stones like thoughts dealt from the dark, wise stones etched with the faces of burrowing owls; all-seeing stones, alone-stones, holy stones.

There are stones that are markers in my life: touchstones that link me to a place and a time. The green cameo stone from Point-No-Point my lover made into a brooch; the sea-witch's stone, my amulet, from Long Beach on Vancouver Island that I have carried with me since 1969, when it washed up at my feet. The first flowerstone I found on the beach at Metchosin. The chunk of green Connemara marble with a snake slithering through its centre, the agate from Rose Spit with a map of Haida Gwaii indented in it, the river-polished stones from Lawn Creek, copper and bronzed by water falling on cedar, stones that bear the fossilized imprints: a drowned woman's hair, a Mayan warrior's profile. Stones I keep in my pockets for the noise they make rubbing against each other when I have travelled too far away from the sea and can no longer hear its sound. The susurrus of the waves pulling the small stones back into the deep.

Each stone, if it could, would speak of rain and wind, the invisible collisions of kelp, musting bones, and driftwood in the dark. They would say a single grain of sand is as worthy of our praise as the open white flowers of the shining summer plum; that we should beware when too much light falls on everything because if we are blinded by darkness we are also blinded by light.

2. Listening to Stones

Ghandi preached for the self-realization of all living beings. He admitted consulting scorpions and snakes on foreign policy matters.

I listen to stones. They, in their silence, have more to tell me than most people. When I give myself to a stone, I am listening to myself, something older than the present organization of myself.

I have wrapped stones in cedar bark, in leather pouches, in strands of tree moss, in the petals of cauldron-like flowers. As I wrapped, I felt myself being wrapped. It was as if I had become the stones whose energy I was containing. As I wrapped I could feel every bruise that may have come to the stone as it was scuttled ashore. What the stone tells me, just through touching: it has nerve-endings, vulnerable parts. A stone changes colour as its moods change. It has a heart, a soul, real eyes to see with.

I found a honey-coloured stone, which resembled a human brain. I left it on the beach because it was too heavy to carry. A week later I went back to the same spot — a beach with a river running through it, and river-polished stones on either side for miles in each direction. I found the brain-stone again, without even looking, as if it had been waiting for me. I had help this time, and brought it home.

It seemed to grow lighter the farther inland we drove, and as I climbed out of the truck with it, cradling it as a baby, and set it on the front porch to acclimatize, I noticed it had a soft spot, like a baby's fontanel. When I touched this spot I felt myself being transported to the other side of consciousness. There I could hear a nurturing stone, a long-lived stone, telling me this: "We come into this world with only the fragile word *I*, an *I* we vainly try braiding into the story of everything else.

3. Stone markers

I dreamed of finding a cave where the bodies of the dead had been placed, row upon row, wrapped in cedar bark, with a stone on that part of them which most needed weighing down. For some it was the legs, others the belly, one the groin. One had all seven natural openings of her body closed with stones. Two had stones blocking their ears; three had stones placed on their eyes.

There is no perfect language for describing the emotional state of anyone who feels the sorrow of so many stones; I lifted the stones and set them into a ring in the centre of the cave, and made a fire. At first the stones shrunk away from the flames, but then they began to speak to me in their own language. Even though they'd seen thousands of years of death, they were not unhappy with their lives.

I sat listening to them and when the flames burned down I put them all back where I had found them because I didn't want to interfere. Not with death, or with history, or with the mystery of mysteries. The stones belonged there, in the blackness of the cave. By touching them I felt I had, with my poverty, bought myself a lifetime of days.

4. Water Over Stones

I chose the house because of its proximity to the stream. I could lie in bed at night listening to the sound of water sliding heavy over stones. Water slipping around, or underneath them, the lisp and hiss of the silt and gravel being freighted towards the sea. There were nights when that sound was enough, and it was all that I would ever need.

He had enjoyed the stream, too, when he first came to live with me. But after awhile the sound changed, the noise of the water rushing around the stones kept him awake at night, while I slept. Instead of hearing the lullaby of the water over stones, right away in tune with it, his mind would begin to replay a judge's address to the jury, or one of the military marches he'd been forced to listen to as a child.

One day he decided to start moving the rocks in the stream, to see if he could get them to change their tune. If he could just change their pattern, rearrange the stones on the bottom of the creek bed, he felt he could change the sound the water made spilling over them.

This man believed that by altering the world around him he would find peace. I said nothing, other than it would be a big job trying to move some of those boulders that had been there since the last ice-age retracted. He laughed and said if he had to he would use dynamite to move them. I felt it was an odd thing to do, blow things up to acquire inner peace, but I had long ago learned not to interfere in other peoples' search for meaning.

5. Displaced Stones

In those inland cities where stones, river rocks chosen for their roundness, are used as decorations — in fountains, in walls or as filler in concrete planter boxes when the flowers have proven too temperamental to live — I feel like a stone out of water, too. I wish I could deliver these stones back to their source, knowing that as they lie here in the fumes, the dust, the gum wrappers and the people going by with Friday on their minds, the stones don't exist, they are in exile.

6. Shape-Shifting Stones

Stones that resemble food: a split baguette; an onion from the downs near Chichester (found on a picnic with Aunt Polly); a perfect beach-stone baked potato; the pie-shaped wedge of mica streaked with chocolate brown from the Kiskatinaw River I keep as a paperweight on my desk.

Holy stones: black stones with two white lines intersecting to form a cross, for my mother.

Intifada stones: colourfully painted, softball-sized stones, thrown at Israelis by teenaged Palestinian boys.

Wish stones: flat soft stones with a hole worn through them. Also called Lucky Stones or (in England) Hag Stones, because they keep witches away.

Fairy stones: stones of weird shape believed to be of supernatural origin and sometimes used as charms.

Lorna's stones: Grey or black with a white band of quartz encircling them. Lorna once admired some that Stephen had brought back from the Charlottes, and now neither of us can go anywhere without bringing back at least one of these for Lorna. I don't even know if she really likes them. They pile up in her garden.

Stones that resemble animals: Sometimes the shape will call to me from across the beach: "Oh," I hear myself say, "a shark! A turtle". And bears: you need a fat, black, long, oval stone for a bear.

7. Stones: A Bestiary

Stones used by shepherds to keep track of the number of animals they had: they collected and kept one pebble for each animal.

Stones used by chimpanzees to crack open nuts they place in depressions in granite outcrops, the Tai forest of the Ivory Coast, Africa.

Stones, a path of stones, as a clue to finding rock wren's (*Salpinctes obsoletus*) stone-sheltered nest.

Stones, a certain rhythmic knocking together of pebbles, used to attract yellow rails (*Coturnicops noveboracensis*).

After the great earthquake in Alaska, fishermen began catching halibut that were full of stones. The fish had felt the tremors and ingested the stones to ballast themselves against the shocks that rocked the ocean floor and reverberated through the currents that bound them. What did the stones feel as they were gulped down into darkness. Did they, like Jonah, have a religious experience?

8. House of Stone

"People who live in glass houses shouldn't throw stones," was something my parents often said. I knew there was supposed to be a lesson in this. But what do you do when the house you live in is made of stone? People who live in stone houses, I learned, are made of shatterproof glass.

I collected stones and brought them home, my pockets stretched out of shape from the shapes the stones made settling in against the new curves of my body. I laid them out on the rough wooden bookshelves my father had made. I had packed all my books into boxes and stashed them under my bed, to make room for the stones. Each stone had a story, and I knew, if I was patient enough, that story would be told to me.

The white pebbles, though, I kept in a different place, remembering another lesson from a book: two children taken into the woods and left there because their father couldn't afford to keep them. Hansel and Gretel leaving a trail of white stones that shone in the moonlight and guided them home. I hid my white stones, smooth and cool as the peppermints I would place under my tongue to make them last, believing, back then, that they might one day be the path back to myself.

I had stones the colour of bruises; I had lilac-coloured stones. I had stones orange as California poppies, the red of the heroin-blood mix. Edible-looking colours: eggplant, persimmon, watery grape. Stones the colour of licked bones; teeth-shaped stones. I had every shade of green, from the black-green of a fairy-tale forest to the wistful green of a beech grove in early spring. Once I found a heart-shaped stone, small as a black-eyed pea, and just as hard; I lost it before I could find a home for it on one of my shelves. I had triboluminescent stones — ones that give off light if you rub, crush or break them.

Some stones had messages etched into them; others had secrets I never could decipher. Some were like miniature land masses, veined with rivers, crusted with mountains, pink, vermilion, burnt sienna. When the stones grew dull I dipped them in water or coated them with a thin layer of oil I had first warmed in my hands — so that they might always shine. I took cold wet river stones and made them into a cairn on a dry pebble beach. I took stones pocked with the spitting of rain and laid them to dry under a slate-white sky. I made myself a pillow of stone, having grown to believe a stone can be a softer pillow than one made of down; in it I could hear the dense heartbeat of the earth. I slept, but each night a slow *splashing splashing* woke me. My tears, hard rain. One stone knows what another stone is crying about.

9. Carved in Stone

Neglect is a stone in a dead man's house. Stones learn by going where they have to go. Stones have no feet but they get there. Stone flies up where your foot was going. Kick the stone, break your foot. Stone only cries when you pick it up. Who looks at a stone to see a stone? Stone flies like a handkerchief, lands like a sack. Gone like a stone in a river. Buried stone is still a stone. Even a stone goes its own way. Get rid of one stone, end up with two. Not big but a stone. Stone parched by the sun, pants at the moon. Quiet as a stone watching a hole over water. No rust on a stone. Listen even to a stone. Ask the mouth, it says: stone. Stone in both hands: what next. Stone tea better than hell soup. Find a stone in the noodles, lose it in the bath.

10. Stone-blind love

What does a stone see as you hold it in your hands?
Who looks at a mirror to see a mirror?
The stone itself is a means to an end, not the end itself.

11. A stone by any other name is still . . .

The English language is bereft of words for *stone*. We have *rock*, and *stone*, both of which, by *rock-hounds* (those who hunt stones, tapping on them with little hammers in the hopes of finding beauty buried inside) are often referred to as *specimens*. In Asian cultures, stone has as many meanings as the word *snow* has for the Inuit peoples of Canada's north.

40 words for stone, from the Korean:

Stones found along the sea or on beaches
Stone with surface resembling an oriental pear
Stone that resembles a rock on the mountain
A single mountain peak stone
A stone with a shelter or overhang
A large stone
A step stone, or a stone having two or more level plains
A pond stone
A stone that resembles an island
A stone that has a cave
A stone with a pattern resembling flowers
A stone that is curious or grotesque, with multiple perfo-
rations or creases
Stones resembling animal bones
Stones resembling a turtle's shell, with white inclusions
covering the surface
Stones found in rivers
A stone that resembles a lake
Stones resembling human beings
Stones that resemble animals
A stone that resembles Buddha
A house-shaped stone
Stones of high quality
Stones of a light colour that look like close views of moun-
tains
A stone with inclusions resembling Chinese calligraphic
characters
A stone that resembles a small spring found on mountain
sides
A stone that has inclusions of white resembling a waterfall

Plains stone: displays a level plain with a mountain or hill
on the far side of the view
Mountain view stone
Stones found in and around mountains
A double-peak or two-mountain stone
Decorative stone
Young stones (those newly collected)
Natural stone: one appreciated for its intrinsic value
Long-lived stone
Nurturing stone
Nourishment of a young stone to make it look older by
watering, hand-rubbing and exposure to the sun
Oriental dragon stone
Mountain range stone (with three or more peaks resem-
bling a series of mountains)
Masterpiece Stones
Garden stones
Beautiful Stones

12. Beautiful Stones

I have planted over the years a garden of flowerstones —
night-black, some smooth, some jagged — with an
alphabet of stars that spell out what it means to be lonely.
It is hard to be lonely when you stand in that garden of
stones, picking magnolia blossoms from where they have
fallen, in the spaces between stars.

Trying to decide where a particular flowerstone should go
— in the rock garden or in my shrine next to the ginger
pot Stephen made me, beside the eagle skull from Skedans,
or the doll wrapped in remnants of grave cloth from
Bucaramunga? I decide to take it back to the beach where

I found it. That's when I begin to see: other stones that I have overlooked because I was too busy looking for what I clearly expected to find.

Agates are the worst offenders, how they distract me from looking for other stones, trick me by their semi-precious importance. When I bring a handful of agates home, I feel I have been deceived. How can a stone be so beautiful it takes away my eyes?

Holding a single flowerstone in the palm of my hand, always this question: *how do we know beauty when we see it?*

13: Shades of Gray Stones

Break break break / On thy cold gray stones, O Sea! A cold gray stone can hoard more mysteries than one in which the light shines through.

I have cleanly-broken pebbles, grey as first light on a west coast morning. Flat stones gray as old bed sheets. Cracked stones the pale gray of a bitter man's face in a mirror. Steely gray like pigeon feathers, pale gray, The gray of ordinary things, gray like pond-bottom mud. Gray as the powdered-covered moth, an oxeye daisy in a roadside ditch. Even bright gray on days when the sun breaks through, smashing the mist with its clenched fist.

14. "There are no blue stones."

A poet writes, "A child will trade a blue river rock for a stick of chewing gum." Another poet responds: "There are no blue stones."

15. Sacred Stones and Profane

East is East: Suiseki (*Sui*=water, *Seki*=stone) is the Japanese name for the "viewing stones", unaltered naturally formed stones found in mountain streams, on deserts, along ocean beaches frequently displayed at Bonsai exhibitions. They are chosen for their perceived resemblance to familiar scenes in nature or to objects closely associated with the natural world.

The essence of *Suiseki*: "The contemplation of a stone as a symbol of nature relaxes the mind from pressures of a complex daily life and allows a person to retain his sense of values. The importance of life in its simplest form is reflected through the beauty, strength and character of the stone."

And West is West: My friend Helen and I found "pet rocks" in a gift shop in Queen Charlotte City: a row of small rocks with cartoon-human faces, glued onto the "bodies" of larger ones. Some had been given hats — jaunty sunhats, base-ball caps — or made to smoke cigars made of long thin turret shells. All of them looked like hopeless middle-class tourists: if there is anything on earth less dignified than a human being on vacation, it is two stones crazy-glued together meant to portray a human being on vacation.

Helen and I decapitated one of these hostage-rocks every time we went to the shop, and released the garishly painted heads back into the sea. We kept up our good work until only a row of dumpy rocks with yellow neckties and red-checked halter suntops remained, apparently unnoticed, squatting headless on a dusty shelf. Over the next months we carried what was left of the body parts down to the sea, and committed them to the depths, knowing they would survive. When you've lived once, they say, you never forget how.

And never the twain shall meet: From an item in Maine Rock Designs catalogue: "Stimulate conversation and recall quiet walks on the beach with these unique accessories for the bar and kitchen. Where else could you find a Sheffield cheese knife set in a 390 million year old hand-polished stone?"

16. Two Miscellaneous Facets of Stone

Stones, seven of them, found at an archaeological site in Syria, an early set of weights, used during the Stone Age.

Stones used to hold down leaves placed as "lids" on top of fermented breadfruit stored in Tahitian stone-lined pits.

17. Healing Stones

Massage therapists place stones (well rounded cobbles) treated with hot lavender oil on a client's head, chest, abdomen and hips. Thumb-sized pebbles are placed between her adjacent toes. "Toe treatment helps the client connect with nature."

Hot stone therapy was used thousands of years ago by the Chinese to treat rheumatism and by Native Americans in sweat lodges. It was also used during the Spanish inquisition, but to a different end: hot stones were placed between a client's toes to torture him.

18. Rebel Stones

A rusty sign on a pole in Northern Ireland, warning, in both English and Irish: "Persons throwing stones at the telegraph will be prosecuted."

19. Ritual Stones

Small pebbles make up the moving parts of rainsticks, used in ceremonies to bring rain to the world's desert regions. Whenever the "sticks" (branches of Quiso cacti with their thorns pounded into the branches' hollow centres, the pebbles inserted and ends sealed) are tipped over they emit a sound resembling a sprinkling of rain building to the swoosh of a tropical downpour.

During their initiation ceremonies, believers in Santeria (saint worship) use vessels made of china and wood containing smooth stones in which the spirits of the gods reside.

The Nenets, a nomadic tribe of reindeer herders of the Siberian Arctic, believe that certain stones are remnants of the gods who have guarded them for millennia.

20. Heart of Stone

I hold my amulet in the palm of my hand, watching it change colour, watching for new faces and symbols to emerge. Sometimes a whale with whiskers appears, a dancing sea-horse, a question mark, a star. If I hold the stone to my ear I can hear more than just the faraway sound of the sea; I hear fields of croaking frogs, clouds blowing from the hills, ice breaking up in the well behind the house, a cat with gray eyes howling beside a graveyard wall.

What does the stone see as it rests in the palm of my hand? It sees the tiny ridges on my fingertips, a swirling weather system of loops, arches and whorls, the distinct signature I imprint upon it, which, like tracks left behind through the silver-gray stones of tundra, can last a thousand years.

I found this stone more than thirty years ago and it has travelled with me ever since, in a leather pouch that has been worn shiny and smooth from so much touching. Every time I return to the west coast I dip it in the ocean so that its energy can be renewed. I always go alone. Sometimes I expect a wave, waiting for me to make a simple mistake of venturing out too far into the deceptive water, to snatch the stone from me. How many winters has this stone been host to the moon and its light, even while I keep it wrapped up, in the leather pouch I am never without, in darkness?

I wish to be buried one day, with this stone in my hand. I hold it in my palm and I imagine my flesh spirited away, my finger bones curling around the stone, and the warmth it will bring me, pulled from the stars.

THE RIVER WITHIN US

TREVOR HERRIOT

FOR FIVE YEARS NOW I have not seen fish eggs in the marsh and flood zone that still somehow manages to breathe life into the river just downstream of Lake Katepwe. I have seen: a gathering of 872 pelicans on the lake just above the marsh; a harlequin duck lost and alone on the weir; gangs of bald eagles lurking in the poplars; mink, several times, bounding over beaver lodges; fireflies winking their soft lights above the bullrushes at dark; all manner of fisher-birds working the shallows, from herons to osprey to king-fishers to cormorants to terns; and LeConte's sparrows, tiny with burnt orange on their cheeks, heads cocked back to sing the marsh alive from the top of signs that say "Fill Dirt Wanted".

The Qu'Appelle, like most of our prairie rivers, is a trou-bled waterway, worrisome to anyone who gives it time or thought. A narrow stream, naturally brown and turbid from clay and loam on its uplands, it meanders across south-eastern Saskatchewan mixing the ecologies of the Northern Great Plains with those of the Aspen parkland to the north. The piece of the Qu'Appelle that I have come to know best is a three-mile stretch from Lake Katepwe downstream to a double-arched concrete bridge that marks where the old highway crossed in a respectful circumnavigation of the marshes and fish-spawning grounds. The new highway slashes across the belly of the wetland where the river channel resumes at the end of the lake, thereby shaving at least three or four minutes off cottagers' car trips to their cabins and resorts. Right next to the arched bridge is the old Katepwe schoolhouse, a brick box anchored to the south-west riverbank where the children of white and Metis families were once schooled in reading, writing, 'rithmetic and river. The people who own the schoolhouse now have no little ones, and so the syllabus of a riparian education on this piece of the Qu'Appelle has fallen to my four children and one mature student tolerated for his ability to rescue mud-hole victims, fillet fish, hoist canoes, and drive cars.

From spring to fall, we walk, swim, wade, and paddle our way along this piece of the Qu'Appelle, the children coveting adventure, me coveting their purity, all of us consciously and unconsciously taking in the river truths that our civilization has chosen to forget. Reading a piece of river is much like reading a piece of poetry. The experience is richer if you can set aside expectations of understanding or mastery and simply remain mindful and open to all that comes your way. This way of knowing, or not knowing, draws us nearer our original mode of engagement with Creation, when learning arose out of humility and innocence, out of a willingness to say "I do not know".

Those are the words that open T.S. Eliot's "Dry Salvages", a poem that, like his river, is a "reminder of what men choose to forget".

> *I do not know much about gods; but I think that the river*
> *Is a strong, brown god — sullen, untamed, and*

intractable,
Patient to some degree . . .
. . . almost forgotten
By the dwellers in cities — ever, however, implacable.
Keeping his seasons, and rages, destroyer, reminder
Of what men choose to forget. Unhonoured, unpropitiated
By worshippers of the machine, but waiting, watching and
waiting.
His rhythm was present in the nursery bedroom.

The god who animates the river moves in a rhythm that was present at our origins, for as Eliot continues — *"the river is within us"*. It is this connection between our origins and the river-god that draws me into the poem: the river is within us, just as surely as the humility of childhood — as individuals and as a race — is within us, for the rhythm of rivers ran through our *nurseries*. If we have chosen to forget this confluence between our youth, our origins and the simple wisdom of rivers, we have forgotten too the source of innocence and the little deaths we have undergone in losing it.

One warm afternoon in late June, as we drove the highway marsh-crossing below Katepwe, I pulled the car over to let my eleven-year-old son Jon and his friend Orion survey their favourite fishing hole. We have had some luck catching northern pike at the mouth of a stream that empties part of the marsh into the river. While we waited in the car, Kate — at fourteen and moving gracefully in the adolescent twilight between the not-yet-hurt and the soon-to-be-hurt — surprised me by suggesting we go wading in the river. It was a good day for it: the river was shallow from bank to bank, save for the occasional hole in mid-channel, and even though the flow was far below normal for June, the water was moving clear and swift over the gravel bottom. As we took our shoes and socks off I looked upstream to where the lake spilled over its weir and into the river. It had been a dry winter and spring and so I was grateful to see any amount of water lapping over the wooden structure.

The four of us stepped into the stream, chilling the blood in our feet and legs, and began following schools of minnows. Orion and Jon found a group of suckers, some a foot and a half long, hanging on the current in the shade of a bank. Mingling with the sounds of their exclaiming and laughter, the voices of someone else's children rode on the wind coming downstream from the weir. I looked up and saw instead of children a young Indian man standing quietly in deeper, swifter water. Built low and broad as a bear, wearing trunks and nothing else, he was thigh-deep in the churning out-flow, bent over with his arms completely submerged, his face inches from the water. As I watched, he pulled himself erect in a smooth swinging motion, one arm extended forward, the other by his waist, drawing something from the river. It was a fish, a bigger fish than I had ever seen in the Qu'Appelle. The distant view, without any sound to confirm what I had witnessed, gave me an odd sense of having slipped into someone else's dream. Man and fish had emerged from the river in a single, easy movement, water glistening on the backs of both. It might have been a dance or a re-enactment of an old story. People don't catch fish that size in their bare hands, not here, not now.

"Did you see that? What kind of fish is that?" Kate put a hand up to shade her eyes.

"I think it's a pike."

I made my way upstream, wading through long skeins of fish coursing just above the river bottom. The next time I looked up I could no longer see the man and his fish. His children, though, had come into view. They seemed to be chasing things in the water, yelling, jumping, splashing back and forth in sudden erratic leaps. Like a group of herons feeding on minnows — lanky, long-legged creatures stabbing at the river between high-stepping maneuvers. I carried on upstream, watching the river bottom and the fish at my own feet, forgetting the man and his monster fish for the time being. As I came round the head of a small island, though, he was standing there beside me empty-handed. I opened my mouth to ask about the fish, but before the words escaped he had reached into the river and pulled it out again in the same slow, rhythmic motion. It broke the surface of the water looking like the front end of a python, shimmering green and lined with rows of pale spots on its flanks. The rim of its flat-topped skull opened into a massive duck-bill, the inside studded with rows of sharp, reflexed teeth. Holding the pike just under the throat and tail, the man smiled, moving his head toward the children, "the little girl, she caught it, eh."

"What kind of tackle was she using?" The question sounded ridiculous the moment it hit the air.

He smiled again looking away from me. "She just used her hands — reached down and grabbed its tail."

There was no response to this. The mouth of the beast in his hands was big enough to enclose the head of a child. This is the kind of pike that swallows ducklings and young muskrats whole, that lurks beneath bridges waiting for cliff swallows to arc near the surface. A wolf in the water.

He put the pike back into the river and it swam away, apparently healthy but a little slow. I asked why he didn't keep it.

"We don't eat fish from here. Some of 'em have mercury lumps on their mouths. Pregnant women aren't supposed to eat the fish from this water." This was a truth I like to forget. The government says it is safe to eat one fish a week. We eat two or three a summer and let the rest go.

As our conversation turned to other things — his children, safer places to fish and a reservoir where his band fishes for food regularly — I looked downstream and saw that Jon and Orion had caught the pike again and were dragging it onto the gravel of an island. I hollered at them to return the fish to the river. "They're going to kill it if they keep that up."

Acknowledging what I had said with a nod, the man replied, "Yeah, it's pretty slow but I thought it was almost, whatchamacallit, revived." We stood there, sharing the quiet river sounds in the middle of the channel, and then parted ways without a word, he to his children and me to mine. I waded back downstream to watch patrol after patrol of the fish we know only as "suckers" — graceful, silvery creatures who got a raw deal when the names were handed out.

I caught up with Kate and the boys and discovered that Orion had lost his shirt. After using it to net minnows, they had dropped it into the water, apparently forgetting that rivers move. We walked down toward the highway bridge to look for it. There were two Indian boys, perhaps eleven and thirteen years old, standing in the shade of the bridge and throwing sticks at something overhead. As we drew near, the younger one pointed at the surface of the river under the bridge and said, "look, is that one of their babies?"

I realized then that they were destroying the occupied nests of cliff swallows, a bird that makes gourd-shaped adobe nests beneath most bridges on the Qu'Appelle. I shouted at them, doing my best to hold in anger, "Hey, you don't want to hurt those birds do you?"

The two boys paused with their sticks in hand and then walked on down the river without looking back at me. By then Kate was on the highway bridge and hollering, "I can see Orion's shirt — it's headed down the river!" While Jon and Orion followed the shirt and Kate's instructions, I climbed up onto the bridge to watch. From the higher vantage I could see one of the Indian boys again a ways down river beating something in the shallows with a stick. Hoping it was something else, something inanimate, I knew it had to be the pike again. The boy dragged it onto the shore and continued the thrashing. The fish was long dead, but he continued to hit it while some older boys laughed and cheered from the far shore. I considered intervening again but didn't. Recalling my own fearful violence with a large pike the week before, I gathered the children and headed for our car.

Jon and I had been out at the old bridge that day, casting our Len Thompson spoons blithely, with little expectation of success, and certainly no clue of the drama that would overtake our morning. Then again, the sight of two small falcons — first a kestrel and later a merlin — each taking an adult cliff swallow from the bridge flock might have been an omen of sorts. The scene, twice played, of chase, capture, death, and retreat, made ritual of the same lethal truth that is enacted every hour in every valley, river, and plain left to the doings of wildness. Each departing falcon — its flight suddenly retarded by the burden held fast in talon grip as

silence fell over the ordinarily boisterous swallow swarm —
punctuated the story's statement: a life has been lost, one
swallow is now without a mate, but the flock remains
despite the sacrifice of one, and a falcon will feed its young.

As I watched each falcon stoop and conquer, though,
none of this came to mind. My response was simple amazement at a "wildlife" spectacle, tempered in the end by a
sense that there was something malevolent in the falcon's
deed. Theories of predator-prey ecology were nowhere at
hand and I was left with the undeniable feeling that the
peace and beauty of the swallow community had been
violated grievously. Uneasy with the sentiment, I shrugged
it off, cast out my line and tried to turn my attention back
to the river.

"There's a big pike out there, Dad!" Jon was pointing
excitedly at a dark hole in the river. I walked along the
bridge to where he stood but could not see what he was
seeing. I made a cast out into the general vicinity, hoping
more for pursuit than for capture, pursuit being so much
tidier, less fraught with life and death complexities. Like
many men I know, I returned to hunting and fishing after
my son came of age, thinking I would pass on the experiences I had enjoyed with my own father chasing grouse and
pickerel. The trouble with hunting and fishing, compared
say to botanizing or bird-banding, is that you end up, more
often than not, having to kill something. And the killing
isn't always at the comfortable distance afforded by firearms.
Birds or fish come in wounded much of the time. You face
them eye to eye, sentient creature to sentient creature, and
there is nothing to do but kill them with your own hands.

First cast the pike struck. I saw it rise to the river surface
and roll, easily a three-footer, perhaps twenty pounds or

more. It went down and I paid out some line, remembering that I had six-pound test on the reel and, even worse, the drag mechanism was on the fritz. To attempt reeling the fish up onto the bridge would be a sure way of leaving a big ugly piece of red and white jewelry in its mouth. Instead, I began drawing it slowly over to the southern side of the bridge where I might be able to coax it ashore without snapping the line. Around each concrete pillar I handed the rod from one hand to the other until I was at the end. From there I gave the rod to Jon, jumped down onto the riverbank and had him hand it back down to me again. Somehow I managed to get the fish onto the rocks. I could see right away that the hook was in too deep to release it safely — I had to find some way of killing it before it broke the line and headed back into the river. I grabbed the largest stone I could find and struck its head but as the rock came down glancing just behind the eye, the fish made a last-minute lunge toward the water, snapping the line and swimming away from me in a single motion.

With the rock in my right hand, I crouched there on the shore, incredulous and appalled at my ineptitude as a killer. Jon, still up on the bridge, was yelling something at me. "I can see him, Dad, he's right under the bridge!"

I fetched another fishing rod with a functioning brake and drag system and climbed back onto the bridge. There it was, holding its position in the current, the hook's leader trailing from its mouth. As hopeless as things appeared I had to try. I let the new hook down slowly into the water just upstream of the fish. On the third attempt, I snagged the loop at the end of the leader — I have no idea how. Again I began walking to the end of the bridge to drag it to shore without breaking the line, taking care this time to pull it further from the water's edge onto the rocks. There wouldn't be another chance. I had to be sure to kill it properly and swiftly, this time with a hammer Jon had retrieved from the car. A knife would have been better but the hammer was in my hand. I winced as the steel thudded into the pike's skull, my own heart racing as its heart slowed to the rhythm of death's final spasms.

The remorse I felt from killing that fish remained with me for days, surfacing again as I watched the boy bludgeon the giant pike. When we hurt the innocent, why does it hurt us too? And, why does it hurt more the older I get, the further I am from my own innocence? Questions I have no good answers for, that may not have good answers. All I could say was that I had killed with regret and as much mercy as I could muster, while the boy seemed to be killing for pleasure. Or was I summarizing the spectacle too simply? We see horrors and react in dumb amazement, mistaking our reactions for truth.

As a child I had killed animals myself with little regret, if any. Once, at thirteen, I wounded a Canada goose in a long overhead shot. It staggered in air, then flew on weakly, angling ever closer to the field's stubbled horizon. I jumped out of my pit and ran to the spot where it had come down. After a search I found it hiding beneath a swath of barley, crouching, wing broken, hoping I would pass by. It hissed at me as I grabbed its neck just below the skull and began, slowly and awkwardly at first, swirling its body in a circle — the traditional neck-wringing method for dispatching a wounded bird. But a Canada goose's neck is as strong as whip-cord and it remained alive after my first attempt. Frantic to get the grisly business over with, I repeated the act, spinning the goose around and around until the body came free leaving me with a bloodied goose head in my hand. I remember laughing at the sight of the head and body now absurdly disjunct, at the reckless ease of killing.

Where is Sam Fathers when a boy needs him? Years later I would read Brody's *Maps and Dreams* and Faulkner's "The Bear" and wonder at all that I had missed in my own initiation into hunting. No sanctifying ritual, no stripping down the self before Nature's great and primeval presence, no prayers or propitiation, and no sacrifice. Instead it was much the same as it had been for my father at the hands of his elders: *here's the gun, this is how it works, shoot when I tell you, and don't ever point it at things you don't intend to kill.* Still, hunting with my father I did learn the habits of birds and hunters, and my bones took on the spirit of autumn mornings in the stubble fields, afternoons walking pastures, and evenings hunkered down at the cattail sloughs, the air moist and heavy with smells of mud and marsh mint. I discovered then that I belong in those places, that death is almost always inelegant, and that killing without sacrifice will eventually wound your soul.

It is this wound in me as an erstwhile hunter that has me confused when I see boys beating a fish to death or when I see a falcon bear a swallow away from the bridge where it nested. And it explains my relief these days when pursuit fails to bring capture. But something in my son wants to see a fish rise and a duck fall, something that I have not entirely forsaken. In me I suppose it is the desire for innocence; in a boy it is the innocence itself.

Only the innocent, a falcon or a boy, can kill innocence innocently. Once we are stung by life, have faced the destroyer without and within, innocence and death change places. We begin to fear death and long for innocence, and the juncture between — where innocence meets death in our adventure and pursuit — loses its savour and gains a cost. Sooner or later, the wages of taking the innocent find us out. It has always been thus, but lately we have forgotten the rituals of giving that once compensated for our taking. To sacrifice is to "make sacred" and it was sacrifice that kept our use of the world holy and wholesome. If our taking is less than sacred, we end up paying the cost in remorse, in the disappearance of the creatures we destroy, and in the unease that accompanies a retreat from wildness.

Most cultures, at one time or another, have recognized that killing without rituals of sacrifice, respect and forbearance is the path to an empty belly, an empty spirit, and an empty land. Hunting peoples acted from spiritually and ecologically-sound principles when they left tobacco at the site of a kill, when they gave thanks, honoured life in death, and offered something of themselves to serve the innocence in their world. The courage to sacrifice — to burn the fuel within ourselves and thereby make sacred the other fires we have lit — strengthens us to carry the tension within a divergent ethic that has us protecting innocence with one hand even as we take a life with the other.

The night the children killed the giant pike, I dreamed of hunting with my father. I shot a grouse and felt again the old elation, the quickening in my flesh unalloyed by qualms or regret. When I went to pick the bird up, though, it came to life and looked at me out of its fear and unknowing. Putting my hand around its neck I could feel the bill and its eye twitch against my palm. I paused, remembered who I was, and let the bird go.

The next morning early I was out driving across the valley bottom in a soft rain. As I neared a piece of the road just south of the river where I had been watching a brood of gophers two days before, something larger moved in the roadside grass. I stopped the car and stared at the spot until it moved again. It was a boy, in his late teens, wearing jeans and a T-shirt, lying down on his back in the brome and sweet clover. I opened the door to the car and something else caught my eye a half-mile down the road where it meets the highway — a small car was upside down in the ditch, wheels still turning from the rollover. I went to the boy in the grass who didn't see me until I was standing above him. "Everything alright?"

His eyes jerked open and he sat up to talk. "Dumb prick . . . rolled the car."

"Let me have a look at you."

"I'm OK."

He was blond, curly-haired, maybe eighteen, and very drunk. Not hurt, just sullen, untamed, and intractable. I asked about his friends in the car. Looking back down the road I could see them crawling out the windows and laughing.

"We're OK, really, nobody's hurt — stupid s'all."

He was afraid I might call the police. I waited for a minute, with the drizzle falling on my shoulders, then said goodbye and turned to go back to my car. As I walked away from the boy, he remembered civilities that adults had taught him and said, cheerily, "But thanks for stoppin' by to check, eh. Have a good day, sir."

Good and bad days will come, but I can recognize the river in a boy, and the voice of innocence freshly back from the shores of death.

CHAIR

ILLTYD PERKINS

Monday, September 17th

Disston Table: 3 hrs. Cut dovetail sliders for extension mechanism, (12 BF QS WOak *@ 8.00/*BF*). surface, joint & thickness all. Cut dovetail slots and inserts. Fussy.* MEMO; *remember to use same ht. on router table to cut strips as grooves. Fit not too good but* OK.

*Walk dog; Visitors — Stibbard (sp??) Bruce & Jane /Joan (?? check !!). 598 2001 Fax 598 2002 (Saltspring) 569 671 2908 (Seattle). Discussion re chairs, poss. table — need for Tgiving (*US*) — hahaha — Christmas maybe? Call back.*

Disston table: 2 hrs — fit dovetails and fasten, bandsaw curves at ends. Sand.

TOTAL HOURS. *Disston 5. Cfwd 64. Total 69.*

On one wall of my workshop under a hanging bundle of templets for a Gimson Ladderback Chair (five slat) are several dusty copied photographs and some postcards. The original photographs came from a variety of books that I've come across over the years. These are the books I would least like to part with, the last to go in any future winnowings, and seem to be those that were not searched out or known by name beforehand. Which makes a convenient excuse for not troubling to look in the first place, but simply to put myself occasionally in the way of chance. Of course, there's always a troubling underthought — what have I missed? — but there's significance enough.

Photograph: "Chair bodging in Buckinghamshire; splitting a cleft log with mallet and cleaving axe".

(The original for this, I am fairly certain, came from "Woodland Crafts in Britain", a book from that brief period of overlap around the Second World War when curious folklorists of cottage industry with bellows cameras could still find and photograph the last generation of men and women working in trades that had not changed in centuries. Now these workers are extinct, though their trades retain an artificial life in rural theme-parks. They can no longer be found in the wild.)

A middle-aged workman with a heavy moustache, the bodger, is standing in a forest making rough blanks for chair legs. Slightly stooping, he is about to drive a long bladed axe into the side of a half-round of beechwood maybe a foot and a half long lying on a large chopping block. He wears thick black trousers with braces, a buttoned-up waistcoat (is that a watch-chain?), a collarless white shirt with rolled sleeves, and a cloth cap.

A surprisingly sinewy arm is wielding (no better word for it) a massive maul, called a beetle. The face of the beetle is worn deeply concave. Particularly interesting are the huge mounds of shavings and waste beside and behind him, as well as the deep carpet of chips on which he stands. A good many billets have been split on this spot, some of which are visible neatly piled crisscross in a tower beside him, where they can dry over the summer.

A little off to one side is his hovel, an A of sticks thatched with shavings and bark, very like Eeyore's house. This is set up next to a young sapling, which has been bent down to almost touch the roof. A rope tied to the tip of this tree goes through the roof and provides the power for a pole lathe — an ancient tool where after a couple of wraps around a billet which is centred between two spikes mounted on a heavy plank, the rope goes down to a treadle. The bodger stamps on the treadle, the rope bends the tree, and as the wood spins on the return spring of the sapling, he thrusts a turning chisel forward to shape a small section of chair leg. The turning on these legs is not crude — beads, coves, raised beads and vase profiles combine in subtly differentiated shapes — now defined and classified by date and region by Antique Collectors' clubs. Investors appreciate these things.

In the foreground are the downed trees which were marked for felling in the winter when the sap was down; only mature trees were taken, distributed evenly over a large area. Younger trees then grew to maturity in the unshadowed clearings, ready in their turn to be felled, bucked and cleft when the bodgers returned to this spot in succeeding years.

All around him can be seen the beechwoods. These are prehistoric woods, stretching then (and still) over the Chiltern Hills. *Fagus Silvatica L.* grows well on the flinty clay of the chalk downs, and probably for as long as there have been chairs to sit on there have been bodgers, itinerant chair-leg makers who worked through the forest in long cycles spanning generations. Beech is ideally suited for its purpose here; it cleaves cleanly, green or dry; it turns sweetly, with a nice polish left from the tool; it's stable, and not given to casting and warping; it's strong, and stains and finishes well, with a pretty fleck in the grain. (It won't do for seats though — too narrow, too liable to split — but for seats there was Elm, in great wide two-inch-thick planks, whorly, knotty, crossgrained, unsplittable, beautiful brown, with an earthy coffinwood smell when sawn, not like any other wood.)

Tuesday Sept. 25th

To Do: call Lorna re Arts Council mtg. + windsor chair repair Hobbs. Fix bandsaw (call re bearing) & sharpen thicknesser. Choir @ 7 — work through Fecit Potentiam. Finish Chair drwg Stibbards & email attchmt.

Stibbards drawings — 2hrs

Polish Disston table — 3rd coat oil. 1.5 hrs. Materials — tung oil (25.00) and 400 grt w/d paper (4.00) Notice scraper mark on leaf. Redo?? Only visible in strong sidelight. Grrr.

Wednesday Sept. 26th

Scrape down leaf Disston Table, resand and oil (??? Dubious move. Stain colour different or what?)

Hobbs chair: to do: seat split; 2 back spindles broken, two missing; back bow broken (cant fix, need new bow); leg tenons loose, stretcher tenons loose, one broken; previous botched repairs on seat; paint splash marks on seat, finish poor to

dreadful. Repair est: 3-400; Called Gary Hobbs. — (9-0028)
OK to go ahead — do by end Oct. (Estimate too low).

Pause, and count your chairs: in your house, apartment, school, office, whatever; in my own house I have . . . how many . . . maybe eighteen, maybe a score. Each one designed by someone, each made by someone. People worked in the bush, in workshops and factories, with tempered steel blades and carbide teeth, powered by diesel and gasoline and electricity; trees were felled, limbed, bucked, skidded, yarded, trucked, floated, debarked and sawn. Timber was ripped, jointed, surfaced, thicknessed, shaped, mortised, steamed, laminated, doweled, glued, clamped, screwed, scraped, sanded, stained, sprayed, lacquered, oiled, waxed, padded, packed, trucked, displayed, bought, carried, used, polished, broken, repaired, sold or given, burnt or lost. Now multiply your count by all the families in houses and villages and towns and cities around you . . .

An index to "The English Regional Chair" by Bernard Cotton lists recorded chair-makers and turners in the Thames Valley, 1700 — 1900. There are over 2,000 names, many centered around High Wycombe. Among them: Abbott, Abram, Adby, Aldersedge, Birch, Boddington, Bridgewater, Caffell, Chilton, Couchman, Didcock, Dimmock, Dobbin, Eeles, Glenister, Gomme, Goodchild, Hazell, Hearne, Janes, Little , Lovegrove, Mott, Narroway, Plumridge (a dynasty — twelve individual entries), Quarterman, Rakestraw, Skull (another dynasty), Stallwood, Stool, Strange, Timberlake, Toovey, seventeen Woosters, and several Youens. As an afterthought I go back through the list; unsurprisingly I find: "Perkins (William), Chairmaker, recorded Census 1851, Stokenchurch, age 23."

Thursday Sept. 27th

OK *on Stbds. chair design (8 Mendlesham Windsors, plainer legs, deeper carved seat. White Oak with yellow cedar inlay lines on back splats and frame rather than boxwood.? Estimate*OK *@ 800.00-1000.00/chair. +* WOakTable *— D end 8 x 4 Gimson extending to 12 with heavy chamfered hay-wain stretchers, stepped octagon legs —* MUST *do by* US *Tgiving Nov 26 (??check date) Advance recd. $2000.00. (Get Wood next week). Slow day — worried about Disston table leaf colour, but not too bad indoors — improved with 2nd. coat. Get J. to call Marni (?) back at* CIBC *re odrft. (8- 5580). Toyota tires in — call.*

Sat. Sept. 29th

Deliver Disston table; looks decent in situ. Marga & Stuart v. happy with table, possibly less with bill (a bit over estimate). But tables last, bills don't.

    Lunch at Moby's with J & N on strength of above.

Picture Postcard: "A Clissett Ladderback Chair in the Leicester Museum".

Philip Clissett was a chair bodger working at home in the village of Bosbury, Herefordshire, near the Malvern Hills, in the 1890s. There he had been making rush-bottomed ladderback chairs since 1838 and is remembered still because he was "discovered" by the London Arts and Crafts movement. James Mclaren, architect, and a friend stumbled across him on a country ramble, "improved" on his designs, and commissioned several chairs, which were then taken up by the Art Workers Guild which had close ties to William Morris. Another London architect, Ernest Gimson, who later founded the Sapperton and Daneway furniture workshops with Ernest and Sidney Barnsley, described Clissett at work: "Mr. Gimson told . . . how quickly Clissett could turn out his work from cleft ash poles on his pole lathe, steam, bend and all the rest. He seems to have made a chair a day for six shillings and sixpence and rushed it in his cottage, singing as he worked. According to old Philip Clissett if you were not singing you were not happy."

(I also rather envy Clissett's way with an order book — when a customer ordered chairs, his name was written on a scrap of paper with the number of chairs ordered and popped into an old teapot on the mantelpiece; then when Clissett finished a set of chairs he reached into the pot and drew names at random until he found one which happened to match the number of chairs he had on hand.)

Ten acres of woods adjacent to Clissett's cottage have recently been acquired by a trust of seven people with an "interest in green woodworking and woodland management". The wood has been renamed, and is now "Clissett Wood", has been designated as "Demonstration Woodland" with the object of "fostering and managing a variety of differing approaches to small woodland management", and is supported by several levels of government as well as the EU. In the summer months short courses in ladderback chair-making and other rural crafts are offered to people on holiday.

Photograph: "The Workshop at Pinbury shared by Gimson and the Barnsleys, c. 1895 – 1900."

A long, low barn with massive stone walls, dark with bright shafts of light coming through deep window reveals, exposed steep rafters and heavy cross ties. In the foreground a work-bench, with deep apron, heavily stained with glue drips and paint. At one end a carpenter's vise of mediaeval pattern. Against the bench is leaning the back of a ladderback chair made by Gimson himself, who had learned the craft from Clissett, these being early days when he occasionally took a turn at the bench: two turned poles, five gradated curved slats and single lower stretcher. More back poles are nearby. On the bench are a few tools: a backsaw, some chisels, a wooden jackplane, but mostly a litter of bits of wood. Handsaws hang on the stone wall, with a rack of chisels by the window. Next to this bench is another, more modern, with an end-vise and bench-dogs for hand-planing; on the ground in front of this are two interesting identical frames, probably oak with very prominent dovetails; they look a lot like the ends for an oak coffer which will have a curved lid. In the background is a very simple lathe for making the ladderback poles and stretchers. Suspended from the roof crossbeams is a large black horizontal pipe — a chimney for heat? — and a single oil lamp with a shade. There are no power-tools or machinery — in fact, no power at all. Only hand tools, benches and shavings, curly long shavings, and no dust. It looks cluttered, busy even though deserted, but clean — clean in a way my workshop never is, even when tidied away with my tools hung and stowed in drawers, all swept and neat; because over everything is always a skin of dust from table-saw, radial saw, drillpress, router, belt-sander, pad-sander, mortiser, grinder and lathe; all under the shadowless glare of fluorescent lamps, curiously known as "full spectrum lighting".

Mon. Oct. 1st

Sidney for wood (oak & yew) for chairs. Need: 8 x 30" 4x4 for legs, 60 BFQS Oak for top plus 60 BF 2 for underframe. Chair seats 60BF 2 and legs. Check yew. 8.00 am Ferry.

Tues. Oct. 2nd

To do: Dentist (clean) @ 10.15
 Begin Table: 8 legs — 2hrs. Raining — light stove. Winter Firewood?? Think about. Choir @ 7 — look at Sicut locutus & thump through.
 Forgot dentist. Humble call. Resched. @ 8.00am 6th.

 Picture postcard: Carving of a Bear by Bill Reid. From the BC Museum of Anthropology.

It's a horrible looking thing: almost life-size, the body is more hyena than bear, crouching hind legs tense with a threatening springiness. The head is huge, with great red blocky teeth. The postcard gives no idea of its massy bulk and weight. In the presence of the real thing it's apparent that the front legs have at some point broken right off along the grain and been repaired with glue and wood-filler. The entire surface of the cedar blocks from which the bear is carved has been roughly tooled with a gouge: the grain of the wood in the gouge-scoops is torn and pitted, cedar being notoriously difficult to cut cleanly. Whenever I visit the bear, I feel perversely that I ought to sand it down, to smooth out the roughnesses in the grain and all the slips and flaws that in pursuit of the perfect finish I'm not permitted to make. I know that its not a good idea to attack grizzly bears with a power sander, but the desire is there: to finish it properly; to make a tidy and workmanlike job of it.

Monday Oct. 22nd

Not doing well; v. slow. the table base OK, tho grain does not really match on the two end leaves. Back to Sidney?? (Oh for matched boards! An English Oak, sawn through and through! Dream on). Two of the eight legs don't look parallel?? How did I screw up like this? Did I check the square on the saw fence?? Maybe the rails got twisted out of square?

Bad day. Total hours 80; Today 3 (headache).

Tuesday Oct. 23rd

Rain rain rain. (Skylight leak back)

To Do: Pick J up from Phoenix after school. Fix choke & wipers Caprice.

Decide to cut out twisted rail, scrap end-section and re-make rail & mortises. Hard to get apart. Some damage, but nothing

*that cant be repaired. Force legs over and clamp and re-glue.
Looks better, I think. Check with square — says its OK now. 6
hrs! Stupid waste of time. Remember to call Stbbs. re advance
— need $$ soonest.*

Total hours, 60.

Wednesday Oct. 24th

*Call Stibbds. Tell them that chairs unlikely by Tgiving but table
OK. Bad 5 minutes. Settle on Christmas. Reprieve. Will send
$$. So . . . work on Hobbs windsor repair. Make bending form
& steam new yew bow. One breakage — drill tomorrow and
finish.*

Photograph: "Waals' workshop at Chalford in the
Cotswolds in the 1920s: Ernest Smith is in the foreground, and Harry Davoll behind him."

(Peter Waals, "a Dutchman of heavy build, slow manner
and sometimes the threat of a dour mood", is not in the
picture, and was by all accounts a frighteningly competent
cabinet-maker originally brought into the business by
Gimson to provide some solid woodworking skills. I rather
think he would have made me feel insubstantial and infirm
of purpose.)

Another workshop, the same heavy deep embrasured
stone walls with flooding daylight, but now with almost a
dozen men busy at individual benches. The walls bristle
with tools — saws, braces, augers — the benches with
planes, chisels, saws and gauges.

The floor again is deep in shavings. Ernest Smith, the foreman, in white shirt, tie, black waistcoat and carpenter's apron is measuring something on his bench. Behind him a completed kneehole desk, quite plain in form but with herringbone inlays along the rails and what look to be nicely fielded drawer fronts; a smoothing plane, probably a Norris, rests on the leather top. Davoll is using a long jointer plane at the bench behind; he is working on another small desk, probably trueing up drawer stock. Half a dozen more men, similarly occupied and dressed, are busy in the background. Next to a finished drop-front cabinet is a powered spindle moulder, one of Peter Waals' concessions to the modern reality of cabinet-making, along with a mortising machine, a thicknesser and a bandsaw which are not visible.

Sometimes, when the work is dragging and dusty and the thought of planing and jointing a heavy stack of refractory oak planks is almost more than I can bear, I think this may be some sort of ideal: a working community, each craftsman responsible for the execution of a single piece; a shared history of technique and style; a common store of large tools for heavy work. An apprentice or two to handle the heavy labour, the tedium of sanding and finishing and the final sweep when the foreman says " Tools away!". To walk or bike to work through misty fields, frost on the grass, the stove lit, the tools sharp. Regular hours, chatter and gossip. Regular wages. A round of beer on Friday nights. Stacks of timber cut from the hedgerows drying in brick outbuildings.

But the workshop didn't last; it couldn't afford to pay apprentices, who wanted proper hours and wages; it could barely pay the craftsmen at the benches, some of whom left to find better jobs elsewhere. There was never a serious possibility that the Morrissean ideals of honest, simple hand-made furniture for the people could ever supplant the affordable mass produced stuff. The furniture made here, like most ideals, remained a luxury available to few, and even at that was probably underpriced. Though the business prospered mildly in its early years, it did not survive Waals' death in 1937; a subsequent fire burnt out the buildings and destroyed his archive of designs.

Friday Nov. 23rd

Frosty morning — ice on pond. Shop warm!

Second coat of oil on Stbbrds table. Looks OK.

Chairs — finish turning 16 front and 16 rear legs. Make jig for drilling stretcher holes (5/8).

To do: measure for stretchers & turn. Assemble bases with seat.

Cut back posts and top rail (curved). Make pattern back splat. Figure out how to inlay stringing??? Shave spindles, turn tenons. Drill for spindles (jig) and front arm support. Assemble.

Hours: Chair 6, table 2. Total hours: Table 80. Chairs 42.

Wednesday Dec. 19th. Rain, dark!

Last sanding on chairs. Look pretty good. Still worried about angle of back and shape of bow. Shave off a tiny bit more in the back curve — better — doesn't dig in small of back. Level legs (give a touch more tilt back), carve date on underside of seats. Last rub down with 400 grit. Vacuum.

Last wax for table; extension mechanism perfect. Top developing glow. Still concerned re straightness of legs.

Hours: 6. Total chairs 160.

One final picture — a snapshot of a chair. In the background my own workbench, some tools — I can make out some clamps and a heavy vise of my father's, a spokeshave which came from his father, and a lovely old Norris smoothing plane which was a gift from a happy client. The chair is one I made several years ago: a typical Goodchild Windsor bowback with carved cherry saddle seat, steamed yew-wood back bow, turned cherry front legs with rather restrained decoration, plain turned rear legs; no rear splat — only hand-shaved yew spindles. I can't quite recall who bought it — I made it on spec., and I think it went south to LA. I wish now that I hadn't sold it: I should have given it to my daughter. It was a nice chair, made for the pleasure of the making, and because there was some leftover wood which suited. It went together without problems, and the angles were comfortable and easy and right. Altogether it was the kind of chair you wouldn't notice in more sophisticated company: anonymous, a decent enough piece of work, nothing showy, just a chair; a little beading on the back-bow and seat front, a good deep saddle with a heavy chamfer underneath to make it look lighter; the oil bringing out the grain of the yew, which needs almost no polishing anyway; by now the cherry will have darkened to a deep chestnut brown.

It must make its own way in the world: it might find a family, or be sold as an odd lot in an estate sale; inevitably its joints will loosen with age, and need knocking apart and regluing. It might break a leg or crack a rung or two, and need major repair; damp may rot the legs so that they need a little trimming — resulting in a curiously low seat height;

or possibly it will fall victim to an infestation of furniture beetle: not much to be done here, probably fatal; and of course there's fire, flood and war.

But then, it's only a chair.

A SNAKE STORY

STEVEN LATTEY

Every Crevisss Givesss a Hisss
To warn uss of a snakess kisss

This is our motto
As we descend
Beneath the massive clifff

SO FAST AND UNEXPECTED, with no warning sound, the rattler whacked me hard in the ankle and then slid off into the bushes, as quietly as she had struck. Such a quiet moment. A stunned, quiet moment. I reach down and touch the innocuous two holes, so clean and surgical. I say to myself,

"You've been bitten by a snake."

I am trying to convince myself of the unbelievable truth. For a moment I think I'm all right, the holes look so . . . so professional. But my heart is pounding and I keep repeating,

"I have been bitten by a snake."

I am trying to understand what has happened. I fall back a few steps and the poison hits me, rushes to my head and staggers me to my knees. I am reeling; only seconds have passed and the poisons are all through me. First, one poison goes straight to my head.

"You son of a bitch I think you've killed me."

"You nasty little bastard I think you've killed me."

I massage blood from the two holes in my ankle to get the poison out of my body. The dark blood comes from deep in my leg, a steady fountain. The two small holes are swelling into a purple welt.

I take my shirt off and wrap it around my thigh but my hands are numb, my fumbling fingers can't tie the knot; can't twist the cloth tight. My legs are numb and I am shaking and so weak.

And the worst feeling of all is this horrible sick buzzing in my head. The whole world begins to buzzz. Got to slow things down. I know this. Got to stop my pounding heart. Slow my heart, cool down, slow now, steady. No time to panic like a fool. This is bad. God, this is bad. Death is near. I am already so awful sick with my limbs going numb and the sound of electrified blood rushing through my head. The sound is driving me out: high volume static inside my skull scorching the pathways between me and my body; destroying what hooks me up with my arms, my legs, my face, my tongue. Oh God, I will die. This feels so very much like death.

Step by step, with a circle of consciousness held like a miner's lamp, like a tunnel of life, steady from my forehead. I must concentrate on each step; that's my only hope.

I tried squeezing the poison out the holes in my ankle; a useless and pitiful gesture. The poison is rushing up my leg.

I tried tying my T-shirt around my thigh. I searched the ground for a stick to make a tourniquet. But the stick broke. Another pitiful gesture against this rip tide of poisons. Useless! I am so afraid. I will fall down in the tall grass and no one will find me.

I must find a centre to hold against the buzzing, whirling world. My miner's lamp is focused on the earth where my feet must go. I say to myself,

"Step by step," and force my legs to swing forward through the growing numbness, like Frankenstein's monster, lurching in this foreign body through the spring meadow.

And I am spitting out this horrid metal taste; gobs of brown down my chin and bare chest: as if I could spit out this poison! What a cruel joke. I am stretching up, away from the ground. I say to myself,

"Your forehead is too far off the ground. You are not this tall."

I am looking at the ground in front of me. But I am too tall. Myself to myself I say,

"The noise is forcing you out."

"You must come back down."

"You are not this tall."

"You are only five foot nine inches tall," my mind wraps around this simple fact like a familiar stone to hold me down in this wickedly changing world.

"You dirty little bastard, I think you've killed me," I say out loud. I am so damn angry.

"Make a goal for yourself. This is bad. The poison is moving too fast. So fucking fast."

My face is twitching. My tongue is big in my mouth like the tongue of a cow. A big slobbering tongue. The top of my head is buzzz, buzzz, like rivers of blood bursting their dams. Like thousands of blood dams bursting under pressure. Like hurricane force storms whirling in my blood. My body is breaking apart.

I think,

"Okay step by step to the trail. Not too fast, just step by step. Keep the centre."

I think,

"If I lose my centre on the trail someone will find me."

"But where will I be if I lose my centre?"

"Oh I will be gone if I lose my centre. I will be gone. Gone. Gone."

I am lonely when I think of this gone place and the loneliness is so big. I am standing alone in this meadow and I will never go home if I lose my centre.

I reel and stumble to the trail. Now up the little hill. Slow now, steady; forcing my frozen legs. Oh, I am so Frankenstein. I stagger to the top of the hill,

"You bastard, you dirty little bastard," is barely a whisper between clenched teeth.

At the top of the hill the world breaks open like a raw egg. I see lightfaces at the edge of my wavering circle. I see faces like light at the top of the hill: *three shining faces.* I call these

faces "hoops" because they have thick rims of Hot Light and they are quiet and empty and deep through the centre.

The faces are way out there, at the edge of our world. Try to imagine dark mouths blowing silver threads, across endless space. The shining faces blow a gentle web of silver threads across a great chasm.

I am standing in the meadow and the threads blown from the faces wrap around me. But I am no longer me. I am a big blue egg, ten feet tall, and the blue egg is filled with a peaceful blue fluid and only the thinnest blue membrane defines its boundaries. The egg floats delicately over the meadow. Barely balanced, ready to burst.

The threads spread across the surface of the egg; *like the roots of a tree wrapping around a rock.* They surround the egg and buoy it up.

The threads are held to the outer membrane by a gentle suction: *like the feet of a water skeeter on a still pond.* This magnetic bond stops the blue egg from splitting its shell.

When the shell splits open and the blue fluid spills out, that's called dead.

When the effervescent blue from inside spills into the big dark blue from outside, that's called dead.

I am the blue egg and I am missing. I am a hole in the centre of a circle of lightfaces. I stand in the centre of a circle of weaving silver threads that stretch out like a loose fabric into the blinding distance. The silver cords reach out to me from beyond the horizon and wrap around me. They cradle me. They float me over the hill.

Through the silver cords I feel the people who love me. I can't see the people, they are too far away, but I am all tied up with the cords between us. The knots are tight. There is no way to untie all these silver threads. The work is too intricate for these clumsy, poisoned fingers.

But I am held in the balance.

At the top of the hill I yell in desperation, bellowing with my cow tongue and wheezing lungs. I can see my truck, way below, at the bottom of the hill.

When I was driving into the park, seems so long ago, I saw people working in the garden of the last house before the park gates. Maybe they can hear me? Maybe somebody can hear me? I am getting desperate. Pretty soon, maybe I can't speak. My mouth is so full of spit. My face is twitching. My jaws clenched one second, slack and drooling the next. I lurch down the hill.

I pat my pocket,
"Don't lose the truck keys." Pat the pocket. Pat the pocket.
"Don't lose those keys."
I am stepping toward salvation, rehearsing in my mind:
"Take the keys from the pocket," pat, pat
"Do not drop them," pat, pat
"Key into ignition," pat, pat
Everything I do now is important, no mistakes.

A man and a woman are walking up the hill.

"Help me, help me, You gotta help me," I gasp but they don't seem to hear. They just keep coming at the same leisurely pace.

"Hey, help me, snake bite." So hard to speak, my mouth full of marbles, my legs and arms flailing, my lungs dragging in air. Down the hill I go. Finally I reach them and throw myself over them.

"You're not joking around, are you?" the man says. The woman is trying to get away. I disgust her. She is scared.

I must look a sight; drunk and raving with poison spit down my chest and a black ooze of poison swelling my left leg. I can feel her reluctance. At least, I think I can. I hold her closer, tighter. I have them both under my arms and she WILL help; I pull them along.

We are nearing the park gate.

Two men are running to me. They know I am in big trouble. They know to hurry. So beautiful to see,

"Thank you Thank you. You gotta help me, I'm dying."

So hard to form the words but I am so thankful they are dragging me and they are trying to save me. I love them. *They are my first reward.*

They drag me into the car. I say,

"Thank you Thank you. I'm dying, we gotta go fast."

So hard to breathe. A hot hand is roughly squeezing and shaking my innards. Bony fingers massage my liver and reach up under my rib cage, taking my breath away. I am twitching all over.

We pull up behind a woman in a little sports car. She is wearing a scarf over her head and she is enjoying a slow cruise by the lake in the Saturday afternoon sun. I reach

over, like a drunk, and touch the arm of the man driving.
I slur,

"Pash the bitch. Just pash the bitch."

He honks the horn and tries to pass. We come to a stop
sign.

I say,

"Fuck th shtop shign. Jush go. Fer christs sake."

He is doing his best and wasting no time but the trip is
taking far too long. Breathing is getting harder. The man
in the back seat is trying to reassure me,

"You're going to be alright," he says.

"You going up Kickwillie Loop?" I ask the driving man.

He says, "Yes."

"Good man. Good man," I say, shivering and rocking,
twisting away from the poison rushing up my body in fast,
shaking waves. I know the shortest way to the hospital. I
know this road. I keep the hospital in my mind. But we are
moving too slow and the poison is too fast.

I am so grateful they are here, these two guys. I keep
touching them to reassure myself they are real and I am still
alive. Touching their warm arms to feel the healthy flesh.
They are not in this foreign place. They do not have this
body that is frozen through the veins, frozen to the core,
cold like death, and a fever raging in the blood; so cold
and so hot at the same time.

They still have real bodies. My body is going away. I keep
moving to see if I CAN move. I keep sucking in air. My
mind is jumping around trying to find a safe place in this
body; some harbour to ride out this terrific storm that is
destroying all landmarks in its path. My mind is jumping
around trying to stay ahead of the storm. This is getting
worse. God I am sick.

We are finally at the hospital, bright white in the spring sun. My legs are completely gone now. I can't move them at all. My arms, I can move a bit. My face is a twitching mass of jumping nerves and clenched muscles. I have a surge of hope. I think,

"We are at the hospital, I'll be okay. They will look after me now. I will live." *This is my second reward.*

But my body is getting worse. Breathing is difficult. The screeching and hissing inside my head is driving me away. I am farther out than I should be. But I will not leave. I will not leave.

"Yes. Oh god, yes, I am here, where they know what to do."

My legs are no good anymore but I can still move my arms. I open the car door myself but tumble onto the pavement. The two guys drag me into the hospital. I have to keep moving. My head is so bad and that terrible hand is reaching up inside me squeezing my innards 'til I shake. Oh what a dreadful poison, shaking me from the inside out. My body does not belong to me.

"You bastard, You dirty little bastard."

I am inside the hospital and on the table cursing and a young face is in front of me a lot. A handsome young face. A kind young face. The nurses, a blonde, strong lady and a darker, more slender lady are playing good nurse/bad nurse to keep me still. I am thrashing about and I am trying to watch everybody to see what they are doing so that I will stay here and not go away from the terrible sound in my head and the pain through my body. I must stay with the pain. My insides are clenched tight like a fist. I must not leave the pain.

And this concerned young man is over by the counter and peering in my face and finally I say,

"Who are you?" and he says he is the doctor and I think how young and handsome to be a doctor and he says,

"You gotta let go of my arm so I can do my job," and I didn't know I was holding his arm. The nurse says,

"Stay still. Stay still for twenty seconds, that's all I need."

They are after my blood but my blood won't come out. They keep trying and trying. I am a squirming creature with the pain creeping up from my belly into my chest. And I am dying when this new wave of poison hits my already wheezing lungs. I am certain of that.

I am looking to the door to see Carol. I want to see her face. I am waiting for her to get here. I have told them my phone number and that was hard; to make the numbers with my face and head so bad and the poison pushing up under my rib cage; and I hope she gets here soon because the poison is rising and I want to see her face. I want to touch flesh that is warm. My flesh is gone crazy with cold that is way deep. I am trying to pay attention to everything around me, I am trying very hard, and then I hear someone behind my head say,

"WHERE'S THE MANUAL?"

And my mind, sitting about ten feet off the floor, laughs and laughs and,

"Oh, my fucking oath," I think, "I'm a dead man for certain."

And I laugh, *up there above the scurry and the worry*; and death laughs with me. After all, this is *his* joke. *He's* quite a joker.

"Where's the manual?" I laugh inside my head.

"Snake bite 101, ha, ha," I laugh inside my head. I am coughing blood now.

I know this is bad. I am not so stupid when they say "you'll be fine". I am spitting frothy lung blood. They lie to me. But what else can they say? I say,

"You lying bastards,"

but do I actually say the words or do I just grunt and snort and twist around. I am not certain. I tell them,

"Shoot me up," and, "Get that stuff in me."

I know I say that. And they try to calm me down and I just keep saying,

"Hurry, fer christ's sake, I'm dying."

Everything is taking so long, so slow. And we are going down the hall and I think we are going up, up, up and I ask the nurse,

"Where we going?"

and she says,

"Intensive Care, we can look after you there."

I am going up but I am trying hard to pay attention and, finally, I see Carol and I think I say "hello" but maybe only with my heart. I have shit my pants and I say I am sorry to the nurses, please excuse me, but I am dying. And later, after my incontinence, Carol is there and I am curled in pain made tolerable with morphine. And she is looking for the truck keys and the keys are still in the pocket of my soiled shorts and the nurse puts on a rubber glove and fetches the keys from my shorts and Carol says,

"Don't bother keeping them, I'll just throw them out,"

And I go crazy. Grunting and twisting, trying to tell Carol she is NOT to throw out my shorts. My shorts with the holes in the ass and the permanent stains in all the wrong places. She is not to throw out my shorts! She has tried before to throw these shorts in the garbage. I will not allow this. My precious shorts!

And Carol knows, for the first time, that I am here. The nurse comes over and says,

"Well, Steven, you could hardly call them your good luck shorts."

She is the plump, blonde nurse. She has a lovely smile. And Carol knows and the nurse knows: don't throw my shorts in the garbage! I want to wear them when I come home. I want to wear them in my little garden. I am still in control of my weathered ship. My battered bark. I am fed through these tubes. I am curled on my right side. The left side is searing pain. But I am not going away. I know where I am. I am here on my right side I am here.

Death from the inside now. I curl and wait. These are dark hours. The venom is tenacious in its cruelty. A vicious, unrelenting attack. I am days tossing in a subterranean ocean. The view is obscured by a murky turmoil of brown and red clouds but what I glimpse between the clouds is brutal.

I see a compressed history of man: a short and nasty history of the world. The centuries are a rosy blur of savagery. I am looking inside my own poisoned blood and every droplet contains another horrid tale. There is no end to the carnage; and the loving drops are so rare. I am a captive witness.

There is no way to turn my head: Avert my eyes.
I have no body: No head, No eyes to turn away.

I think I am way up in the northeast corner of the hospital, on the top floor, near the roof. When I roll over the machines make a terrible noise because my heart is beating so slow. I can see the low numbers and the sharp graphs on the noisy machine. I roll over and over groaning and wake to hands kneading the terrible knots in my shoulder; eyes searching my eyes; eyes begging my eyes to come home. And then down I go, one more time like a man drowning; *into the yawning caverns beneath the massive cliff.*

They move me to another room. I am still in Intensive Care but I am not directly in front of the nurses' station; I have my own curtained cubicle. The nurse looks at the bag of piss hanging at the end of the bed and says,

"No more blood in your urine,"

And this is my third reward. I am coming down. I am coming home. I am so tired against my pillow.

They move me to the common ward and Carol comes to see me and we are talking and I say,

"You know, when I was up in Intensive Care,"

And she laughs at me and says,

"Intensive Care is not *UP*, it's on the main floor."
I say,
"No way."
She says,
"Yes, darling, Intensive Care is on the ground floor."

But in my mind I have been on the top floor of the big white building, in a hushed, computer-lit room, riding out the storm.

Who would have thought that such a little stroll over the ranges; *the ranges I have walked since childhood, the buttercups and sunflowers and lupines, the bucolic backyard of my boyhood dreams;*

Who would have thought I would wake a sleeping snake to strike with no rattle to warn. A snake would strike me unawares, as I surprised her in her slumber dreaming of field mice to be devoured.

And the walk towards the snake! The fateful walk. Carefully and carelessly chosen steps; a stop and a go; a left and a right. I started down the trail to Kalamalka Lake and changed my mind and decided to climb the ridge so I could look down from the cliffs: east into Deep Lake and south down Kalamalka Lake and west over the range hills to Terrace Mountain.

I picked my way carefully up the ridge. I could have gone anywhere. I walked directly to the snake. *We were fated: an ill-tempered snake and me.* There is a certainty about the whole affair. This is an affirmation of life? This is a demand? What is this? My teacher, the snake, is ruthless.

Death is always at our shoulder but only rarely does he tap us with his stick. And tap so firmly! And such a stick! Such a primordial stick. A stick so deeply rooted in the most ancient soil of our selves.

I am horror-struck again and again, on a bad night. The silent moment. What the eye sees so clear and quick, and the oafish mind is so slow to comprehend. The oafish mind is in denial, refuses to believe the simple celluloid image from the eye. The whack of triangular head against the ankle. The quick, quiet slide over the feet and one, two, three undulations and she is gone, as quiet as she came.

My eyes record the surgical precision of two hot holes. My mind reels back two, three steps. Mind and body moving together in harmony for this last moment. They reel back together in disbelief, in denial, in horror: *an ancient pose that becomes my midnight loop of film.* A moment recorded on the walls of caves and in Egyptian drawings. I am brought, ankle to fang, to these old reptiles. These ancient ones who have stricken fear in our hearts since first we bit the apple and tasted pleasure in the flesh.

Even then, when we were young fallen angels and new in our flesh;

Even then there was the snake.

It's three months since She got me. The worst damage is gone from my body. My leg was black and swollen to the top of my thigh, but that's gone. There was a ring of blisters like a chain around my ankle.

Now, I'm tired a lot and the soles of my feet are sensitive. I walk on baby's feet, sore little baby's feet. I am a true tenderfoot. I go "ouch, ouch" as I walk across the kitchen floor and back to my couch to rest. My leg aches where the fangs sunk in. There are hard bruises deep in the flesh.

I am very happy to be writing this letter and to be able to tell you my crazy story from the comfort of my own tired body. I am happy to rest and drink in the quiet green with my eyes. I sit on my porch with my hands on my knees and look into the garden. I shudder with pleasure in every breath. I barely move. Electricity still rushes like a black flower up my spine. I laugh easily and cry too much.

I cannot read a newspaper in public because I cry at any brave story (man saves children from house on fire) or heartfelt story (boy buys bell for church). I cry at any brutal tale or pitiful tale (prostitute drug addict murdered). I always have my sunglasses near at hand. It is as if I have no skin.

I am startled by shadows at the edge of my sight. I am easily frightened. I think death is following me. It's better I stay away from people right now.

I feel as though I am straddling two worlds and understanding neither. I am a dichotomous chimera. Two rivers, one hot and one cold, flow through my tender, little feet.

This story is for the three beautiful shining faces blowing silver threads across endless space that kept me coming home. They are the hoops, the wheels, the weavers, the mouths that blow

the gentle winds. They are the persistent ones; the ones that stay at the edge of our world until the bitter end. They are the lace bridges over the pit.

I had to tell death to go fuck himself. If death should suddenly be at your side and you don't want to go with him, you have to shout the bastard down. You have to dance for your life. You have to show that laughing sonofabitch you want to go home to your little garden, your beautiful little garden. This is no time to be polite.

Death will win, in the long run. He knows and you know. But not now! Come and take me later when all these silver knots will be easier to untie. My body won't be frozen with this poison. My mind won't be cursing the injustice. Come later, when I am more ready.

Then, death will be like a dream I had so many years ago.

In this dream there is an old man sitting in a simple room.
He is a beautiful old man with a big grey beard
And he stands up in his simple little house
And he turns so he is facing the chair he was sitting on
He steps up onto the chair
And the chair becomes the first step in a stairway to the top of the wall.

The roof is gone and a night sky is now the roof.

He climbs the stairs to the top of the wall,
Steps into the night sky,

And is transformed into a golden fluid that floats into the heavens.

The golden fluid
Splits into smaller and smaller droplets
And is absorbed into the dark distance.

Gentle. Peaceful. Elegant. Eloquent. Noble.

GETTING INTO THE
CABRI LAKE AREA

TIM LILBURN

1

GO TO LEADER AND STAY AT THE HOTEL across from the elevators if it's too cold to sleep on the river flat just north of the Estuary townsite. Estuary is west and north of Leader — you'll have to pass by it eventually: only five houses or so left, two last summer with trucks parked in the yard, another one, a white bungalow set off to the west, nearer the river, owned, rumour has it, by an American hunter who turns up every fall or so. Anyway the Leader hotel. It's old, smells of cigarette smoke climbing through the ceiling from the small bar below; you could read the paper through the sheets. On the weekends, they have a buffet in the evening and morning. The town is doing well; a number of people there work at the PetroCanada plant at Burstall, a forty-five minute drive southwest. If you arrive on a Friday night, visit the Swiss men's store owner the next morning before you set out: lots of stories and some interesting merchandise aimed at the Hutterite colonies in the area.

Come down into the river valley past the old Estuary cemetery and the abandoned town: the large cement rectangle rising out of the grass with the square hole is the old safe of the Standard Bank. To the west is Bull's Head, an odd-shaped bluff facing the confluence of the Red Deer and the South Saskatchewan rivers, deep water at the base of it, good for fishing. The ferry runs irregularly; if the man is on the other side when you get there, he'll see you and come over. Turn right when you've risen out of the valley and the valley's elm thicket and follow that crooked road east into the sun — just as it bends north you might see some clouds of white dust heaving up in the distance, winds coming off a large alkaline plain. That's where you're headed, Cabri Lake. You'll have to walk from the road, a long walk, cropped land, pasture, marsh, then a stretch no-one seems to be doing anything with — I saw a large coyote there last year: its head made me think at first it was a sheep. If you do manage to get into the land around the lake and talk to anyone about this, keep your directions to the place as vague as these.

2

The ascesis of staying where you are: your cell will teach you everything. I don't know anything right now. The land is there and I am here and I don't know anything. I keep lifting my mind to the light and peering in: nothing. My sort of people have always been moving through — Alberta looks good these days, they say, maybe BC — tuned to the anarchic flux of capitalism, a little too bright, a touch off plumb, with eagerness.

3

The acme of speech is language that carries the knowledge of its inevitable failure inside it: the word cannot be circumscription; it cannot name; it can't even confess with accuracy. But it still loves — helplessly — the world and so walks alongside it; it says what it loves is a red, red rose, says it's a sunset, dusk over a river, and names nothing with this, misspeaks what it points at but hears and reports a moan far inside the speaker. Such language can't identify what it wishes to name but it somehow manages to achieve a greater proximity to that thing by opening a reaching emptiness in the one who uses it. This is desire's speech of course: beauty makes you lonely; beauty gives you a sweat of plans; thick, multi-layered beauty makes you homeless. You must have close to nothing for any of this to happen, though, it seems. Lyric language is a companion along this way — it doesn't know what it's saying. The highest theology, pseudo-Dionysius says, is not definitional but hymnal: praise and wait for something to take you in.

4

Another interesting place to go is the sandhills around Senlac, half a day north — sleep in the truck at the regional park there, close to the Alberta border, or take a room at the Sunset Motel, fifteen dollars a night the last time I was a guest. There's a large Manitou Lake at the north end of the huge range of treed-in dunes a little south of Neilburg, strange mounds surrounding it; there's abandoned towns scattered throughout the area, Artland, Winter, lots of community pasture and dirt roads, a place that could rub away a large part of your name. Most of the pasture is contiguous; once the cows are off, you could walk, you sense, forever.

5

Language that doesn't know what it's doing; desire that doesn't know where it's headed: I spend most of my time listening and hear pretty well nothing. Maybe I've run out of gas, maybe (against all odds) I'm being obedient to the last real thing I've heard. A good place for breakfast is the Senlac cafe. In the beer parlour at night: oil workers and long time drinking buddies, some just returning from a brief retirement from the booze. The Anglican Church in town is definitly unused; it looks as if they might open the United Church for funerals. All of the names of the streets have a British ring, Hastings, William; the cenotaph at the centre of town has a plaque for The Great War with eleven names on it.

6

This is what I can tell you about Cabri Lake: a large salt flat surrounded by high brown hills. My guess, based on the size of the alkaline clouds the wind was lifting, is that it would take a day to walk from the south to the north end — likely you wouldn't find any water as you went along: grass, grass, grass, then the big salt pan, then more of the same toward the horizon. I didn't get any further than the hills to the south of the white flat; that's where I saw the coyote ambling along, tilting its nose now and then until its nostrils were parallel with the wind; it didn't see us, didn't even appear to be wary — who comes into these parts anyway?

You will find water, though, as you approach the southern hills, a couple of ponds, a stream and a salt marsh: take the east hill side of the stream as you move north: the west shore just leads you deeper into the marsh and that sort of mud can be unforgiving. I saw a godwit in one of the ponds you pass as you come toward the marsh.

There is a story that a large human effigy rests in the grass flats around the empty lake, or possibly in the surrounding hills, well hung, ecstatic; someone saw it from a small plane thirty years or so ago; there was a newspaper report I vaguely remember. Your chances of finding it on foot are about nil. Or maybe it was seen further east in the Great Sandhills; I haven't heard any mention of it in a long time.

7

The Western contemplative tradition, Plato to Weil, and from even before Plato, his Odyssean, shamanic precursors, is a simple story: desire and having nothing; being scrapped down until you can see beauty; beauty itself scrapping you down. The idea is to get to positionless responsivity: utter permeability guarded by the temple dogs of collection and division. This, say the dogs, is genuine advance, that is plain cleverness. This pair comes toward you out of anamnesis, an experience of beauty so strong it makes you half crazy and gives you the strange sense that you remember now some early, perfect time when you simply *knew*. Such an experience both ruins you — you will be ever unlike — and is the way home. They will come up to you, the two dogs of discernment, friendly but not domesticated, animals out of the forest, and snuffle your hand. This in itself will be disconcerting.

Be as available to the right sort of daemonic exigence, says John Cassian, as a bit of down is to wind: the pure state is erotic nomadism: take this position as, at least, heuristic, and let it work you down.

8

Two other good places to get into are the valley of the Frenchman River, east and south of the Cypress Hills, and Rock Creek Valley in the East Block of Grasslands National Park, both on the northern limit of the Missouri drainage. Go in winter if you can; you will be able to walk the river: the ice is thick enough except where beaver chew protrudes and has made a small rapids. There you'll find open water even in the coldest weather. Listen to the river and you will be able to make out these places, current gurgle, current splash against ice, or simply follow the trail animals have made, mule deer, coyote, fox: cougar, people say, are moving east along all the river valleys, tracking an explosion in the white tail population.

Don McKay and I came in here three or so winters ago, mid-February, and spent one day slogging through waist-deep drifts down the coulees along the valley sides, having left our snowshoes in the truck: the valley top had no more than half a foot of snow on it and we thought we could safely forget the shoes. The next day we walked east along the river, coyotes crying in sequence along one side of the valley, across the flats and up and along the other side in the afternoon. We found the odd kill site but not too much else appeared to be happening in the wide white place. When you come you can stay either at the ranchers' bar in Val Marie or the re-fitted convent on the southern edge of town. The bar in Mankota is a good place to eat if you are coming in late from the east.

It would be difficult to get into the East Block in winter; there's only a track from the gravel road and, of course, it's not plowed; few people go there so no trail would be broken. You might make it if the snow cover is very light; close all gates after you pass through: someone is wintering cattle here and would appreciate your courtesy.

But if you can't get into the East Block in winter, try late summer after the golden eagle brood has fledged on the bluff where Rock Creek bends south. Come in from the north; that's the route everyone takes, but maps show there's an entry on the west though I've never felt eager to try it. In the winter, that way wouldn't be worth the risk; people don't seem to live out there, and there simply would be no way in; you could get stuck in drifts and freeze. A sudden rain in summer would strand you in gumbo. But it might be worth a try in dry weather. Do a little shopping in Rockglen before you come down this way and plan to spend a few days. The hills around are badlands, clay with rich grassy drainage clefts; there are antelope through here, some impressive rubbing stones. Camp anywhere.

9

Being in a place demands a practice: it isn't tourism or Romanticism; things aren't laid on, nor are they occultly given; here the practice is putting yourself out there and walking. There is almost always a wall of fear to pass through as you undertake an exercise like this, the temptation to turn the truck back at Rockglen or Wood Mountain, to stay not so long, to forget the whole thing. It's nervousness around being *atopos*, I think: beauty-wounded, being culpably away from others, wasting time: maybe what comes up to you won't be friendly. Push a little on it and the blockage yields somewhat. Do what you can; walk and see where it gets you. The walking, though, is not an instrument, not a means to arrive at some autochthonic accord; as you walk, you are already as there as you're going to get, though you hardly feel this: the reeling, toppling condition of always wanting is as close as anyone gets to grace.

10

The Cabri Lake area — I think I'll go back there this spring, or maybe I'll curve up to Gronlid and Arborfield at the edge of the Pasquia Hills Wilderness, thick aspen bush on the border of the northern forest — I've been wanting to stop in at Arborfield for years. I don't know what I'm doing, and when I listen I hear nothing, my ear embedded in a blank on the band. I'll go where this not-speaking, not-hearing urges: it's a thin road but little else is on offer. Ruby Rosedale community pasture, West Montrose community pasture: walking in the fall is best when the light is exhausted, one of the last hawks circling overhead, too high for hunting, and the distance seems to drink you a bit at a time.

HONEY SONG

BRIAN BRETT

"The poetry of earth is never dead:
When all the birds are faint with the hot sun,
And hide in cooling trees, a voice will run
From hedge to hedge about the new-mown mead."

— John Keats
On The Grasshopper And Cricket

"THEY'RE SINGING THE QUEENLESS SONG," the old beekeeper said. He's a tall, thin, cranky man who doesn't appreciate fools. Once, he was a mathematics teacher, but the bees took him. These days he's an angry swarm of advice, educated in too many things, and made bitter by his knowledge. I go to him for instruction. After he's finished lecturing me about my inadequacies and the failures of my generation, the secrets spill out — he's generous despite himself, begrudging his desire to communicate the stories of a lifetime among insects; they'd spoken to him for too many years, and I think he's ashamed of his own species.

My first hive was troubled. Even an amateur like myself knew it, so I stuffed the entrances with foam and bound it with the rubber inner-tube loops he'd given me, humped the whole hive onto my pickup, and drove out of my east field down to his cluttered yard. As soon as I dropped the tailgate and we stood listening in the humid late afternoon, he knew she was gone. A hive is always talking to itself. This one was humming grief. There was no queen, and no eggs that the workers could remake in time to save its life — the hive was dying, its last survivors wandering mournfully on the empty combs without purpose. I needed a new queen.

Anyone who raises bees, I very quickly learned, begins to speak a new language. Some of us begin to learn what language means.

I knew something was wrong by the way they were flying, their slowness. A sick hive can even smell different. The odour of the combs, their colour, their density constantly vary — sometimes red, sometimes blackish and thick, sometimes pale and fluid, or even crystallized like sweet amber. One hive, depending on the luck of seasons and predators, may contain as few as five thousand bees or as many as fifty thousand. Resting my hand on the lid, I felt a low, sad thrumming. A healthy hive is aggressive if disturbed. At the first commotion a couple of guard bees will leap into the air. If I bang the hive around an angry mob will kamikaze towards me.

When a bee stings, the exquisitely designed barb, resembling a futurist sculpture, its tip composed of two lancets jabbing alternately, sucks itself under the skin, until the apparatus snaps off at a breakaway point and remains in my pink flesh, venom sac attached, shouting an olfactory warcry, as the bee stumbles away and dies, self-eviscerated. Gunga Din style, the released scent of the stings will constantly direct the attention of new warriors to the ambush site. After seven minutes the venom sac reactivates and pumps in another shot. I've watched this often: the sac seems alive, still obeying the commands of the hive. Even if the advance guards do not sting they will seize me with their mandibles and dab me with a volatile odour that will lure other guards, who will decide if I am worthy of the sacrifice, since every sting means suicide. Only the queen can sting repeatedly.

After I brought my first hive home, I used a handheld water sprayer to inhibit their activity, and because I didn't have a proper mask and gloves, I moved slowly and carefully. Bee stings have never bothered me, so I assumed I could absorb a few. Bee venom is a miraculous substance, composed of seventy-six chemicals which interrelate in a way that amplifies their effects. A tiny stinger slightly thicker than a pin can kill people with sensitive immune systems.

"Deadly poisons," according to Ovid, "are concealed under sweet honey." Bee venom has been used for centuries to treat diseases like arthritis and multiple sclerosis. Some apitherapists have suggested that acupuncture originated from studying the effects of bee stings on various parts of the body. I know a local man inflicted with MS whose wife uses tweezers to place live bees on his spine's key acupuncture points every two days. He showed me his back once — symmetrically inflamed by the healing stings. Paralysed down one side when the disease first struck, he now jogs past my gate every morning, with just a slight numbness remaining in two fingers. The effects of bee-sting therapy vary wildly. Other people report that it merely helped them wiggle their toes. For someone inflicted with MS that is encouraging news. Hope is huge in the world. There is a sad film of paralysed victims praising the venom as if they'd discovered the fountain of youth.

What first drew me to the bees was my own arthritis. I stung myself for several weeks. It was a curious experiment. Since my wife is allergic, I kept my bees, given to me by a local beekeeper, in a spare bedroom in our barn. I'd sit on the bed, and lift a bee out of the jar with a tweezer and hold it against the skin. The rush was brutal, especially by the time thirty barbs hung like tiny fetishes from my knees. The adrenalin would speed up my metabolism, pounding my heart against my chest, my skin alive with sensitivity, and I'd leak an awful-smelling sweat that, enthusiasts claim, allows the toxins to ooze out. Then the stings had their second pulse. After fifteen minutes I began removing the stingers. They slid out easily if I got the angle right. I'd sit and gaze at the water jar where the crushed and drowned bees had been put to death (it can take a bee many hours to die after releasing its sting), and I felt overwhelmed with the sadness of the world. During the next days my sweat ceased to stink, and I found myself more energized. I lost weight. The pain in my knees went away. Then, after six blessed weeks, the pain returned, so I gave it up, yet I decided to purchase some bees anyway. I guess you could say I'd been stung.

For most people bees are scary. There is something about tiny crawling creatures that instinctively repels us. Seals are cute: bees, spiders, wasps — we squash. Through a microscope, though, or in a close-up photograph, they are lush, brilliant, seductive creatures — as beautiful as tigers and flamingoes.

The bees arrived in a small crate built like a miniature hive, called a nuc (pronounced nuke), short for nucleus.

A variety of the dark Italian breed, they were quiet, flying around me, but not aggressively while I lifted out the removable frames and inserted them into the "super" that would be their home. My border collie sat curiously at my side, studying this interesting development at the farm. Like most working dogs she wants to know everything in case one day she has to control it.

Then I wiggled the frame with the queen and her attendants, trying to release it from the sticky propolis that's formulated out of tree sap and used by the bees as a glue. When I lifted her frame, a boiling mass of bees surged towards my face, and for a moment the world went black as they filled my mask's screen with their angry bodies. I brushed a few away, noticing that the collie was now mysteriously standing at the gate two hundred feet across the pasture, having time-shifted there instantaneously. I slammed the frame into the super and ran for it, pursued by the angry mob. They could tell I was an amateur and decided to teach me a lesson — they didn't give up the chase until I was a hundred yards away, my skull lumpy with stings.

No one knows yet how to describe a hive of bees, or for that matter, the other great social insects, termites. The swarm, like a human body, is a living, thinking creature. Maurice Maeterlinck in the early 1900s talked of the "spirit of the hive", later terming it a "superorganism", a theory allegedly plagiarized from the South African entomologist, Eugene Marais, earning Maeterlinck some vicious personal attacks. It now appears possible both men unconsciously cribbed the concept from another scientist. Lately, Thomas D. Seeley has begun describing the hive as an amoeba —

contracting at night into the perfect 93-degree heat of its own womb and during the day flowing out as far as five miles, morphing sensually, mumbling almost absentmindedly to itself, holding multiple conversations while it feeds and breeds.

One of the ways social insects organize themselves is through pheromones. Odours that give instructions. The honeybee queen secretes some from her mandibles and rubs it all over her body, while her soothing attendants massage her, picking up infentismal amounts of the secretion and oiling their own bodies with it. Then other bees rub this pheromone onto their antennas, and disperse into the hive, passing it along. It's estimated that the workers will pick up a trace of the queen's reassuring smell on their antennas at least once a day.

Marais, in his *The Soul of the White Ant*, described several experiments involving the communication system within termite hives. He noted that a certain Dr. Bugnion split a nest with a metal plate several feet wide and high, large and thick enough to prevent odours and sounds from passing through, isolating the queen on one side. The termites continued working. They built perfectly matching arches on opposite sides of the plate, as if it wasn't there, or the queen had somehow guided them. Only after he assassinated the queen did confusion fall upon the workers who knew immediately that she was gone — on both sides of the plate. Overwhelmed and sad, the hive collapsed and died. This is why good pest specialists will merely seek the queen and remove her. The work ends when she is gone.

I often wonder how animals mourn. On my farm, I meet death often. The other day a peachick died of blackhead. The peahen crooned beside its body until I buried it. Then she went off and reclined in the sun beside an azalea bush, her brown wing extended protectively over her last surviving chick. With bees, I've never noticed any mourning over slain individuals, though the act of stinging will bring a vengeful host. What do they know of death? They certainly mourn when the queen is gone.

I sited one of my hives by the pond, shielded from the wind by a pussy-willow clump, the earliest feed for bees, along with the native plum. There's also a nearby weeping willow, under which we bury the animals we have loved. Each animal is buried with a stoneware or raku pot I made in my studio, the graves marked with distinctive stones found on our farm. There's the canary, several cats, two dogs, peacocks, and Stonewall Jackson, the old horse who died last year.

Though a farm can be a murderous place, the death of a horse marks you for life. We were lucky enough to find him immediately after his stroke. Semi-paralysed he was thrashing on the ground, trying to rise. Death always tells us how inadequate human language is, our incredible, stupid inarticulateness — I ended up holding Jack's head in my arms, telling him it was okay to go. At first I'd attempted to revive him. I was so huge with sorrow that I somehow managed to lift him onto his feet. A horse down on the ground will inevitably die, and he knew that too. I leaned against him as long as I could, bracing him on his trembling legs. What crazy creatures humans are. He was just as crazy, shivering, swaying, holding on, until we both folded up and were back on the ground.

Now he's under the willow, and thistles grow above him. The bees love his grave and its thistles, flying over it on their long dangerous journeys, noticing or not noticing it, mourning or not mourning their many dead. The hive is safe there, surrounded by page wire to keep out the sheep, and whatever marauding animal might desire honey. Humans also walk off with hives — a good hive will contain up to 200 pounds of honey, which can translate into a fair amount of money, and larceny is common to the human heart.

On a cool wall in a cave in Valencia, an eight thousand year old figure dangling on a rope fills his honey basket while angry bees swarm him. Those were the days of extreme honey-collecting. Surprisingly, they haven't changed much in the remaining wild sectors of the world.

Honey hunting, in Asia and Africa and South America, remains a significant form of collection despite the introduction in the nineteenth century of the rectangular, Langstroth hive. By discovering the "bee space", the small gap bees will not fill between honeycombs, Lorenzo Langstroth made removable frames within interchangeable "supers" possible, instantly converting beekeeping into a major industry. Before then, hives were generally kept in logs, pottery jars, or wicker skeps covered with mud, and the bees had to be killed or driven off with burning sulphur in order to collect the honey, making it a far more dangerous and less productive enterprise.

In Africa, a bird, the Honey Guide, *Indicator indicator*, lures humans and apes to hives by laming its wing, calling and struggling towards the sweet reward. The grateful honey robber must always leave a comb of honey for the bird, otherwise it will never return again according to legend, or worse — lure the robber next time into a carnivore's den.

More fascinating than how we find our way to the honey is how the bees find their life-sustaining nectar. The hive communicates; therefore, it must have a language. Yet for years we regarded ourselves as the only creature with the capability for language. Even before gorillas learned sign language and parrots how to count, the question of animal language exploded when a pioneer botanist devoted himself to the words written by the hive. Karl von Frisch spent decades studying swarms, painting bees, blinding them, gluing up their scent organs, calmly but scientifically torturing them in a thousand original ways as he dissected the living body of the hive until his sometimes diabolical researches pointed towards the dancing bee concept of language.

After a bee finds nectar or pollen, she will return, and dance. The dance is like a fever that travels contagious through the darkness of the combs from one forager to another, each passing along her description of the sun's position, the variety of flowers, their location, and the quantity. These directions are so precise they can guide a bee over lakes and hills and valleys and around trees, to the food supply, sometimes miles away. Honey has a direction.

This is how Frisch defined one dance — a bee inhales the nectar into her honey stomach, and dusts her legs with pollen; then returns. She is met first by guard bees, and then by storage bees. This is where the song begins. If the flower is close, the honeybee will perform a simple round dance, calibrated to the direction of the sun. One of her greatest directional tools is her eyesight. The eye of the bee is composed of thousands of ommatidia, or smaller eyes, hexagon shaped, which orient her colour vision towards the blue end of the spectrum. Red appears black to her, or shades of grey, though she sees hints of blue, green, yellow, and orange. Viewing video reproductions of the bee's point of view is like taking a roller-coaster ride on acid. Her kaleidoscopic world is a mosaic of stark colours, reminding me of the way badly functioning fluorescent lamps can sometimes make a room eerie; combine this with the helicopter antics of her membrane wings, and you get a vision of the world that would nauseate most of us. Her eyes also act as polarizing filters, lining up sunlight in a directional sign of little rods all pointing away from the sun. As long as there is one tiny hole in the cloud cover, the bee will be able to take a perfect position, and add that to her location memory. Above her two compound eyes, she also has three photocell-like eyes which can tell time exactly by the intensity of sunlight.

When a bee flings herself from the landing board, helicoptering up to eye level, she is a highly charged erotic creature. Her duty is to ravish flowers. She has dreamed the dance of direction and the high frequency legends uttered on the combs, the pheromones, and the whiffs of pollen and nectar brought back from the fields. She zigzags, finding her course, tapping down to confirm pheromone footprints on the leafs and grass left by earlier foragers from the hive, seeking the carnal heart of the flower. Various kinds of solitary and social bees have developed lovers' tools to suck up the nectar and stimulate the anthers dripping with pollen. Some tumble through hidden trap doors, wallowing in pools of nectar and are then stroked by pollen-bearing hairs. All this voluptuous activity fertilizes the flowers and feeds the hive. Some bees are greedy, ripping their way through the petals to bathe in bright wombs of nectar and pollen; others are more devious lovers, slipping into the petalled sheaths and vibrating their wings at exactly the right frequency to make all the pollen come tumbling down. In the world of the bee, dinner and sex are simultaneous.

Most flowers have adapted to the bee, trading their nectar for pollination. Many have what's known as nectar guides or honey darts, brilliant strikes of colour pointing the way like incandescent road signs. In others, like the Meadow Cranesbill, the lines are almost invisible to us because the petal reflects ultraviolet light. To the bee it is pale with stark black lines. The bees are a loyal bunch and will almost exclusively exploit a specific kind of blossom when it is in season. This is called flower constancy.

Today, in the smouldering heat of the afternoon, I watched my Shungiku Chrysanthemum being over-whelmed by a drunken flock of foragers, luxuriating among its velvety red and yellow petals in an orgy of debauched feeding. They are rewarded not only with nutritious pollen but nectar, the high energy drink containing sucrose, fruc-tose and glucose among other blessings. Nectar is so potent and the bee so mechanically efficient that it has been calcu-lated a single bee could travel 2 million miles on a gallon of nectar. I gaze ruefully at my old farm truck and dream of honey-fuelled engines.

Over the years, flowers and bees have evolved to fit each other like gloves and hands, creating monstrous, needy combinations; especially with the notorious odour deceits and tricky, visual traps of orchids — other mutations have led to long-tubed flowers and long-tongued bees dancing together in the sun through the fields of evolution. There's a species of quasisocial bee, the Euglossa, a beautiful crea-ture, often metallic blue, bronzed or burnished like gold.

It's said the males are driven wild by the scent of a specific orchid which they madly attack, and then smelling each other, clump into a writhing group called a lek. The female Euglossines ignore the orchids but the motley crew of seething, brilliant males will catch her attention and she will dive among them and choose her mate.

The life of the hive, like most farm life, is female. Males serve for stud service or slaughter. In the hive, every worker can become a queen — if she is fed royal jelly — but one suffices. Multiple drones hatch in the spring. Big and useless they roam about like bumbling bachelors, enjoying the run of the combs, living in luxury, sometimes moving from hive to hive, always accepted, awaiting their moment of glory. The young queen will make several preliminary flights, scouting her countryside, perhaps to remember it for the dark years ahead. Then one day, she will leap out of her hive and take to the air, releasing a jet trail of pheromones, emitting a chip-chip-chip sound as she makes a delighted lunge for the sun. So loud is her cry, so strong her odour, males will find her from hives ten miles away. Those that fly the highest and fastest will reach her in the "drone zone", a hundred feet above the ground. A few beekeepers claim they have heard the snap of their tiny genitalia as they break away from the queen and tumble to the ground, ripped apart by their one act of copulation. Sex and death at high altitude.

Once is not enough for a queen. She will accept several drones, ensuring the genetic diversity of the hive, each one having to lunge higher and harder in the ecstatic nuptial flight, lushly described in Maeterlinck's *The Life of the Bee*, perhaps the most romantic passage of natural history ever written.

After the nuptial flight she returns triumphant, trailing her lovers' genitalia like streamers, and the failed drones revert to their old bachelor mode, mumbling about the hive while the female workers grow more and more annoyed at them, until late in the summer they are evicted. Some will fight bitterly, uselessly, the relentless females shoving them out of the hive, suicidally stinging them to death if they resist, heaping up clumps of bodies on the landing and tumbling them down into the waiting mandibles of the voracious wasps. The slaughter of the summer drones occurs yearly.

Sometimes, I enjoy standing in front of my best hive, watching the foragers navigate around me as if I were a tree trunk. They walk out onto the landing, and lift up vertically, take a sighting, and then wander off on their missions. One of the fortunate and necessary facts of bee life is that, resembling human society, they have their own solitary independents, the visionaries who refuse to take instruction. Like daydreaming poets, they seem as lazy as those mysterious ants that run up and down a line, never packing anything — yet they are the foragers destined to discover new sources of nectar. They also must tell lies, because occasionally they are not believed. One diabolical researcher released some foragers at a feeding station placed in a boat in the middle of a lake. Few returned to the station from the hive, though they accepted another offering to a control group fed from a station on the shore.

The landing board of the hive usually displays a small phalanx of guards, waiting like Sumo wrestlers at the start of a match, ready to fight off wasps, beetles, bumblebees and sometimes, mice or birds or bears. A few foragers arrive like drunks after a wild afternoon of partying on the hallucinatory offerings of the flowers, but generally, the returning foragers, if loaded down, dive straight for the entrance. With their full honey stomach and stuffed leg baskets called corbicula, they are pack horses of the sky. Work is the business of their life. In order to make a pound of honey a single bee would have to fly three times the circumference of the planet. When you consider the amount of honey in a single hive, the reason for all the activity is obvious.

As each worker matures, from hatch to death, she goes through many changes, first secreting wax, manufacturing and lining the hexagonal cells — a nearly perfect shape for both storage capacity and strength; then she morphs into a storage bee, or sentry, and finally matures into a forager, the most dangerous stage in her career. Despite the traps I've hung, and the odd, lucky gumbooting of a low-flying wasp into oblivion, a few exhausted foragers fall to the grass in front of the landing, where the yellow-jackets lurk. The wasp will rush over and begin slicing up their victim before she can regain the air again — she is eaten alive and struggling, the full honey stomach a tasty snack that Shakespeare recognized, since he has Bottom say: "kill me a red-hipped humble-bee on the top of a thistle; and, good mounsieur, bring me the honey-bag." Entomologists believe that bees began their evolutionary separation from wasps due to a similar habit. Dining on aphids, they noticed that some were made sweeter by the nectar they collected — a wasp's version of lamb with mint sauce. They gradually came to prefer the nectar straight up, and thus the bee was born.

If the forager makes it to the landing, she is greeted by the self-important guards who give her a quick smell and frisk. She will often lift her butt in the air and fan her wings, delivering an odour account of herself and her journey, and regurgitate a treat of nectar to an overly aggressive guard. Approved, she enters the darkened hive and passes the pollen to a storage bee who quickly packs it away. Then she regurgitates her nectar into the mouth of another storage bee. This is where the miracle of honey occurs. The storage bee compulsively flicks her tongue coated with a film of nectar, air-drying it and introducing an enzyme, invertase, which allows the final conversion into honey; it's then packed away, and fanned constantly, to reduce the moisture level further. The bee literally deserves the Homeric epithet, honey-tongued, for it is on the bee's tongue that this glorious gift of the earth is made, the sole source of sugar in the western world until only a few centuries ago. Nutritious and bacteria resistant, honey was also used to treat human wounds before the age of antibiotics.

Once the forager has off-loaded, she begins her dance.

If the flower is far (more than a 100 metres), instead of the round dance I described earlier, she will perform what we call the waggle dance, this time figure-eighting the direction while wagging her butt. The bees touch antenna and the feverish dance sweeps through the hive. Decisions are made. The swarm focuses on a single source. Flower constancy gives them the fussiness of poets, deciding they are all postmoderns this week, romantics next, until they are glutted with their source, and move on.

Using the calibrations from her polarizing eyes and internal clock, a honeybee dancing for thirty minutes is so accurate she will adjust her dance several degrees to allow for the movement of the sun. Longitude and latitude are an inherited trait. Studies have found similar displays in the stingless bees of South America and the fierce giant honeybee of Asia, the *Apis dorsata*. These enormous honeybees prefer living in the high reaches of the Tualang tree where, 250 feet above ground, they are safe from the honey-seeking sun bear. Notoriously aggressive, their immense hives have been utilized by bandits who gathered swarms and adorned their treasure caves with them.

The *Apis dorsata* was said to be a Hindu handmaiden, known as Hitam Manis or "Dark Sweetness". The Sultan's son fell in love with her, but she was ejected from the palace by the Sultan because of her commoner lineage. A melee broke out, she fled, and she was somehow speared to death; then she magically transformed into a giant bee.

Much later, the prince was gathering honey in a Tualang tree. He hacked up a hive and called for his cowhide basket to be lowered, but when it arrived on the ground, it was filled with his own dismembered body. This was his punishment for using metal on the hive, for it was a metal spear that had pierced his beloved, but she had mercy on his brutalized body and rained a golden shower upon the basket and he magically reformed into a living prince. She did not have the same opportunity herself, living forever in her magical hive, surrounded by the hives of her handmaidens. She lives on today, though the giant bees are becoming endangered due to deforestation — their legendary honey hunters, a dying tribe. The *Apis dorsata* were responsible for the infamous "yellow rain" that fell upon American soldiers in Vietnam, many of whom remain convinced the Viet Cong were using chemical warfare on them. It was only bee shit.

The Asian honey harvesters continue to use wood and hide and bone to harvest the nectar of the handmaiden, and they refer to themselves as her handmaidens, or Dayangs, hanging in the dark of moonless nights, hundreds of feet above ground where they hammer the hive with a burning torch, creating a "shower of sparks" which the enraged and dangerous bees follow to the ground while the chanting Dayang carves out huge combs of honey with the scapula of a cow, gathering as much as a thousand pounds from a single tree.

The *Apis dorsata* is the only bee that dances in daylight. A returning forager lands on the sunny side of the long, wide, flat, single-combed hive, where she dances exactly to the vertical if the nectar comes directly from the angle of the sun, or whatever degree to left or right it lies.

Everywhere in the world the bees dance their poetry of food and life.

This is where the story begins again. Like any story it is about more stories, and how they begin. Frisch's theory about their language was so astounding that after a few initial years of disbelief, scientists applauded him. The dancing bee hypothesis was too beautiful to reject. It soon merged with the canon of human thought. Frisch won the Nobel Prize in 1973. Yet while Frisch was being crowned, a stubborn scientist named Adrian Wenner denied the dance that was evident to every researcher who looked into hives. Instead, he claimed each foraging bee rediscovered the flower by smell. The dance was only ornament, not a real language. Other studies demonstrated that released smells from the Nasonov gland, and pheromones, also provided clues, along with the high-frequency sounds of the wings of a dancing bee.

Wenner burst upon the scene like a young Cassius Clay, "floating like a butterfly, and stinging like a bee". Soon joined by Patrick Wells and a cluster of other "rogue" researchers, his theory was greeted with such outrage that most scientific publications refused to publish him or his supporters. In the years since, Wenner and his colleagues have developed good arguments for their odour hypothesis, despite the virulent reaction of the mainstream scientific community, which acted as if it had just been stung. Since they were unable to publish much in the journals, Wenner and Wells artfully performed a classic example of lateral thinking. They wrote a witty book about the dustup itself. *Anatomy of a Controversy*, published in 1990, was greeted with rage and praise, but slowly, many entomologists have begun to find truth to their arguments, or at least the odour discovery. Probably the most hilarious aspect of this debate, is that for years, one disagreement revolved around a single study based on the behaviour of 37 bees. If nothing else the controversy exposes the lunacy that can inhabit scientific research. Also interesting are their accounts of similar, bitter denouncements of other scientists by their peers, until history eventually proved them correct. A little more than a century ago the greatest scientists of France scoffed at the notion that burning lights fell randomly out of the sky. These days we call them meteors.

As with many heated debates, neither side is entirely right. The truth takes all of them. The real answer appears to be an amalgam of dance and odours, not only from the nectar itself, but of the bee's own making, and includes high frequency sounds of up to 250 cycles per second. They dance, they sing, they rub their wings, they release strange and wondrous scents, they seek random directions. Their language and behaviour is more complex than we are capable of imagining.

Sometimes, when I am lying down, resting in the orchard with my girls humming around me, I watch them dip and seek and dream and hang out at the landing pad, and I think about language. I long ago realized we only have rudimentary ideas about how communication works, though we constantly insult other creatures, insisting they are unintelligent because they can't or won't communicate or behave according to our standards. (Parrots are notorious for their devious corruptions of intelligence tests.) It's not a question of whether animals communicate or whether they have structured languages, it is whether our understanding of language is sufficient.

Western thought, over the centuries, has regarded language as exclusive to human society, yet as our knowledge evolved so did our definitions. We intrinsically want to judge "the other" — what we don't know. There are always barbarians at the gate, or savage beasts, dumb brutes. Now we are discovering the dumb brutes are us. Savage, blinkered creatures, only recently have we begun to leap beyond our own point of view, literally into the skin of *the other*, unravelling the intricacies of how so-called primitive societies work. The term primitive people has become over the last fifty years an intemperate, racist remark. Many "primitive" societies had a more mature understanding of language than our self-proclaimed advanced western society, driven by the myth of the scientific method — that flimsy, flawed tool we use to convince ourselves we are logical.

Throughout history rogue philosophers, poets, and prophets have offered alternate versions of communication theory, but they've been mostly ignored. During the last century philosophers and semioticians (Umberto Eco) and deconstructionist critics (Jacques Derrida) undertook a serious dismantling of the simple surface of the way we communicate, though most deconstructionist thought is buried in a stubborn academese that itself blocks communication. Still, many of their ideas are now part of the lexicon. During the last thirty years we've begun agreeing that communication is a dreamlike thing, hard to label, it's only limitations the arbitrary ones we load onto it. If anything, the world of communication theory is approaching Ezra Pound's shifty definition of poetry as "intense language".

Language is all around us. Yet we cannot hear or see because like the characters in Kurt Vonnegut's *Harrison Bergeron*, we shade our eyes, plug our ears, stop up our noses, cover our skin. Of all creatures on the talking earth, we are perhaps the one most incapable of a real conversation with our world.

But the talking of the earth goes on, everywhere. Iguanas converse using push-ups. They flash the bright skin flaps under their chins, bobbing in complex patterns that tell stories of hot rocks and love affairs. They perform manoeuvres awkwardly labelled with dumb, cute terms by researchers — the "funky jerk" or the "shudder bob", a courtship dialogue full of walking gymnastics. Sometimes they, like us, sing soliloquies to themselves. They have regional dialects too. An iguana from Mexico might not entirely follow the conversation of some sweet lizard from Arizona — though they have a syntax and grammar common to each other — so they can probably make out fine.

Recent work on the Caribbean reef squid, *Sepioteuthis sepioidea*, has shown they conduct conversations using colour. They are constantly talking, wooing, celebrating, congregating. Every night they disperse into the deep Caribbean to hunt and feed, then return at dawn to shallow "hot spots", squid clubs, where they party and yak. They have extraordinary control over their colour, using patterns, hues, intensities, as words. They can hold two extended conversations at once. One side of a squid can be busily threatening a male on the left, while simultaneously flashing its elaborate courtship conversation to a female on the right. How many guys can do that at a singles bar?

The dialects of killer whales are readily distinguishable, as well as dolphins, prairie dogs, and sparrows. Prairie dogs allegedly have different words for different human beings. One of them is: "He's got a gun!" I've heard ravens use their version of that same word after they killed one chicken too many at my farm. They disappear real fast if they see me haul out the hardware, since they've already learned from other, more aggressive farmers what rifles can accomplish. Amazonian parrots not only have unique dialects, but those living on the borders of different ranges can speak in both dialects. Bilingual parrots? Too bad we aren't intelligent enough to understand what they are saying.

Deconstructionists, semioticians, philosophers, and biologists are working towards a new vision of language.

Information theorists are formulating concepts such as "maximum entropy", the number of signals in a communication system. According to this measurement, the iguana has an index of 13. English has 1,908. The honeybee, 25. Another measurement calculated is "evenness of a communication code", a crude method for deciding on efficiency of gestures or sounds. When this measure is applied to human beings, we are a useless 0.01. The chickadee is 0.14, and lizard language an impressive 0.48. That's talking!

I have the reputation of being a great storyteller, according to some people. The truth is I am a lousy talker. I've heard tapes and watched films of myself. Yet I communicate easily. My father was a Cockney potato peddlar born within the sound of Big Ben, and I inherited what little of the gift I have from him. I grew up on the road, selling potato dreams to people who didn't know they were hungry. When I stand back and analyse my stories, I realize that I, like most of us, use more than words. It's not the stories at all, but my unconscious manipulation of the space between people, eye gestures, hand movements, time, the weighing of emotions among creatures in an enclosed space. I probably change smells when I am talking. I am inarticulate by our common standards; instead, I'd like to think I talk like the bee talks.

Great, invisible stories are being written all around us, every day. Who knows, if we don't destroy ourselves and the earth first, we may evolve enough to learn the language of the world. I think not. It's full of ineffable secrets and mysteries, and we are ignorant, silly creatures. While tiny bees are creating legends of giant boulders and lost fields with gleaming nectar-full flowers using their symbolic and creative vocabulary of smell and touch and light particles and dance and squirted chemicals and high frequency vibrations, we are still arguing about whether they have a language. As Paul Newman once said immediately before being shot to death in the classic cult film, *Cool Hand Luke*: "What we got here, is a failure to communicate." The blind, destroying greed of our species dumbly rolls over everything in its path while I sit in my false little oasis of an organic farm, surrounded by the monstrous machine of globalization and big business. We take everything beautiful and use it to Wal-Mart our lives. Nothing is safe. We have used bees in warfare, pouring their honey on our wounds. The Japanese in WWII glued microscopic messages to bees in order to send information through enemy lines.

For thousands of years the Americas thrived without the honeybee. Pollination was accomplished by solitary bees: the bumblebees, mason bees, carpenter bees, stingless bees, etc., Meso-Americans learned how to extract small quantities of honey from a few varieties. A century ago in North America the natives looked up in horror at a sky full of "stinging flies", for if the swarm came, that meant white farmers like myself were not far behind, ready to colonize and change the land. Now in this new world, I am also endangered. A farming community that consisted of 96% of the population a century ago is down to 2%. Farmers spend more money on chemicals than machinery or seed. Their pesticides are poisoning millions of bees, already suffering from other introduced pests, foulbrood, varrora mite, tracheal mites. The wild honeybee is near extinct, the large commercial apiary operations floating in a plethora of chemicals. These islands where I live used to be the last land in North America that produced organic honey. Then a holly farmer illegally introduced bees from the mainland, so he could get more berries, and better prices for his Christmas crop. The imported bees were infested with varrora mites. That was the death of the wild honey-bees on Saltspring Island.

Yet I stubbornly continue to learn the world of the singing bees who inadvertently teach me small, new lessons every day while going about their lives. Civilization, communication, progress, these are the myths we tell ourselves. I don't have faith in them any more, but what's left of the natural world, though it is often brutal, I can still love. Resting my hand against the hive I can feel the thrum of their conversations, and I dream about all the magic going on inside. Sometimes, on my better days, I think that language is just another word for the poetry of the earth.

WILDERNESS AND
AGRICULTURE

JAN ZWICKY

WHEN THE WILDLIFE CONTROL OFFICER from the county came, he confirmed we had a problem. "They'll take every tree within 200 yards either side." He was eager to set the dynamite and watch the dams go up but, having grown up hunting north of the Sault, he didn't like the part of his job that required him to kill beavers: "don't shoot what you can't eat." But there was no point blowing the dams, he said, if you didn't kill the beavers too — they'd just rebuild, usually overnight. He told me, trying to reassure me I think, that they weren't particularly "nice" critters: he'd seen them use traps, with the bodies of their dead kin still inside, to repair dynamited dams. Thinking about it later that evening, I couldn't decide if that made them sinners, or saints.

There was no question I could get the county to do the work. Our fords had been destroyed, the banks were being seriously destabilized, we were losing fences, and, arguably, the whole horse pasture might eventually be cut off — all of which meant your tax dollars could be spent on our farm, to control beavers in the name of "conservation". And while it was nice to be invited to think of myself as a responsible eco-citizen making hard choices for the greater environmental good, it was pretty clear that accepting that invitation was just a way of simplifying and obscuring the real issues.

In the first place, there was my hopeless prejudice in favour of the trees: trees are so beautiful. Think of what they do with light and wind, think of their patience, their vulnerability. And these particular trees — mostly poplars — their slimness and whiteness, the exquisite lisp of the aspens, the perfume of the balsams in late spring. Their presence along the riverbank, and the colonies in the east pasture and on Baldy (the oxymoronically-named hummock in our south field) defined the visual presence of the farm. They constituted its margins which, as Wendell Berry has observed, are not only ecologically important, but essential to a certain sort of rhythmic pleasure humans take in landscape. (This is not to say landscape without obvious margins can't give us aesthetic pleasure, but that it gives us pleasure of a different, or sometimes more subtle, sort.) Anyway, no question that without the trees our farm would not be as easy on the eye. Nor would it look "the way it had always looked" — that is, exist visually as a symbol of historical permanence, of my present's continuity with my past.

So: very convenient for me that the course of "conservation" turned out to be the path of least resistance. I could tell I wanted to be beguiled — but precisely because I could tell that, it wasn't happening. So what was wrong with wanting to save trees? Why was the coincidence of private desire and public policy making me uneasy?

Once I'd put the question in those terms, the answer seemed pretty obvious: both were serving the interests of a certain *way* of appreciating nature, a way that was arguably opposed to the interests of nature itself. Or to put it another way: the trees stood at the interface between wilderness and agriculture — me on one side, the beavers on the other — and my unease stemmed neither from private scruple nor ecological complexity, but simply from the fraught, puzzling nature of that interface itself. Western Europeans and their postcolonial descendants have, in the last hundred years, discovered that it won't work to proceed as if agriculture had *no* relation to wilderness: but we still have very little idea what that relation should be.

One of my friends once remarked, as though it constituted a *reductio ad absurdum* of environmentalists' views, "Why, they're even against *agriculture!*" Er, but — when you stop to think about it, what's so crazy about that? The suggestion that humans require agriculture — or at least the current North American version of it — to survive as a species is patently false, while the suggestion that it has been responsible for massive environmental damage both on this continent and elsewhere is indisputably true. "Well," my sceptical friend might continue, "that's not a problem with *agriculture*, it's a problem with the way it's practised, with its scale." But this begs the question of what other scale it might be practised on. European, colonial and postcolonial agriculture are not phenomena independent of patterns of settlement and exchange, economies and trade, population densities and, nowadays, corporate profit. To change the style and scale of agriculture would be to change culture itself. What my friend wants is what we've got, with maybe the odd design modification. What environmentalists have seen is that desire is not sustainable in the long run. In a way, my friend is right, it *is* the scale, not the fact of *some* human culturing relation to land, that's the problem; but to change the scale significantly would be to change everything else about the way we live.

What is wilderness? Typically, we think of it as "unsullied" nature, nature in her "natural" state. But push on this a little and two further assumptions emerge: that there are (or have been) portions of the earth completely unaffected by human activity; and that human activity is, by definition, "unnatural". I'm not so sure about either of these claims. I agree that a great deal of what my own culture does and advocates in relation to non-humans is wrong, unhealthy, and disruptive of relatively stable cycles of growth and decline. I agree that its practices themselves fail to exhibit the complexity, rhythm, and balance that are hallmarks of "natural" processes. But none of this has to do with what is essentially *human*: it has to do with a particular ideological inheritance.

And, although I agree with Bill McKibben that because of my culture's insensitivity we are now, globally, confronting "the end of nature" — PCB's concentrating in the Arctic, the plastic loops from six-packs washing up on remote atolls in the South Pacific — I don't see how the ecological truths underlying its demise weren't ever thus. What members of my culture are coming to realize is that the planet constitutes an astonishingly complex whole, comprised of many disparate but interacting sub-systems, themselves comprised of smaller sub-systems. But this fact has not been *created* by environmental crisis: it is something that environmental crisis merely makes more visible. As long as there have been humans on the earth, their activities, like those of all other beings, have in more and less subtle ways affected the smaller and larger ecologies in which they have occurred. Because PCB's are poisonous, and especially because my culture has produced a lot of them, we are now *aware* of "human presence" where we were not aware of it before. But the atmosphere has always dispersed, carried, and concentrated various human by-products. If human activity is "unnatural", and therefore defiling of the wild, there hasn't been any true wilderness for at least 200,000 years.

"Wait a minute," someone might say, "you're missing the point. Nobody's going to deny humans have always been mixed up in their environment. But there's something different in kind about the abominations introduced by twentieth-century Eurpean warfare and industrial capitalism. Of course 'wilderness' doesn't mean 'no campfires'; but it does mean 'no strontium-90'." Does it, though? Is it the bare presence or absence of certain substances — however miniscule, and however produced — that determines the presence or absence of wilderness? (Suppose lightning, striking some dust gathered for ceremonial purposes, produces a molecule or two of strontium-90 . . .) Well, no: quantity *is* a factor — and, it would appear, so is motive.

These observations, taken together with the inevitability of ecological interaction between humans and their environments, is why I want to argue that wilderness depends not on the absence of human interaction with the land, but rather its quantity and style. Wilderness exists, I'll suggest, in greater or lesser degrees wherever we allow communities of non-humans to shape us at least as much or more than we shape them. (Of course, if you think no such openness presently occurs anywhere, and has no possibility of occurring in the future, you'll want to cast that last sentence irrevocably in the past tense.)

Trevor Herriot, in his searching and perceptive chronicle of the Qu'Appelle, comes at the same issue from the other side:

> Most of our problems began when we hammered our hunting spears into ploughshares. From that point on, it has been one valley after another — Euphrates, Nile, Ganges, Rhine, Seine, St. Lawrence, Mississippi, Hudson — evicting the local hunter-gatherers and pastoralists, replacing them with farmers who soon multiply, filling the valley with a civilization that venerates the tiller's short-term residency, calling this "settlement", while dismissing the hunter's long-term residency, several thousand years of seasonal migration and ecological congruency as mere "nomadism".[1]

It is not, in other words, human culturing that destroys wilderness: it is the manner of that culturing and the attitude behind it. Many human societies have negotiated — and in places, I'd argue, their remnants continue to negotiate — the border with the non-human world in a way that has permitted and permits both sides to flourish: thinning and weeding, aerating and fertilizing, burning and irrigating, all with the aim of increasing the health and complexity of various plant communities and thereby their own harvest. What they have tended not to do is break the sod, or clear-cut, or fish with dragnets; they have not, in general, aimed to eliminate whole communities of native species in order to promote dependence on non-native cultivars. Above all, their populations have stayed relatively low in relation to the population of the wild species they live, and lived, among.

Viewed from this perspective, *wilderness* and *agriculture* are not dichotomously opposed terms that, between them, exhaust the possibilities. Rather, it begins to look as though *agriculture* is a term that mediates between the non-human and its exploitation — a.k.a. industrial logging, corporate fisheries, or, more generally, agribiz. The Greek word we usually translate as "wild" is *agrios*, which means literally "of the field"; but it is formed from the word *agros*, field, which is the root of our word *agriculture*. In this etymology the wild and the cultivated come from the same place, the field that accommodates and sustains them both. Agribiz, by contrast, sees the field only as the arena of short-term capital profit. In such a field, there is no room for wilderness, nor, for that matter, culture in its broader sense.

But what does this mean for our farm? Surely we're not engaged in agribiz? We've got less than half a section under cultivation, low till, no pesticides, herbicides, or chemical fertilizers, we use small equipment . . . Yes, but: there wouldn't be a beaver "problem" on sw32-57-08-WS, if the land those numbers designated wasn't "in production", if the poplars and spruce and willow hadn't been cleared from everything except the banks, hummocks, and steep hillsides. The beavers could take as much as they wanted and the course of the river wouldn't be "destabilized" if the place were still wild. There'd be plenty of balsam and aspen left for the occasional human, passing through, to enthuse over.

Is this, then, the direction of the solution: to campaign for a reduction in human population, a return to a more nomadic way of life, and in the meantime to put the farm back down to trees and let the beavers be? Perhaps. But even this proposal — maybe I'm just kidding myself? — seems to bear the stamp of insufficient subtlety and complexity. It forgets that individuals, too, are ecologies of history and desire, as much as cultures. While my planetary-thinking head recognizes the ecological wisdom of the suggestion, my locally-acting heart isn't sure it's up to it. My grandfather *homesteaded* this place. Neither my mother nor my grandmother could imagine putting it back to trees; I can barely imagine it. And I don't just mean the landscape. I mean all that labour, the struggle it represented, the hopes that fed it, the violence it required — there's something fantastic about thinking it might all have been a mistake. More difficult, I find, than wondering if the species itself might be an evolutionary dead end. It's more like trying to think through whether you yourself should have been born.

And here's something else. I can't think of a "nomadic", non-agribizcious society that, as a female, I'd be willing to choose over the one I already belong to. This could easily be because I haven't read enough, or it could be because what I've read has been filtered through English-speaking patriarchy. I know there's a wing of feminist analysis that locates women's oppression in the advent of private property, which itself seems to have begun with ownership of herd animals. But if what I've heard about the sexual division of labour in many Palaeolithic cultures is correct, or about the political privileges of women, even in societies that trace descent matrilineally, I am not at all sure that reversion to such a way of life — even if it were possible — represents an ideal I could aspire to. There's a link between the Enlightenment's vision of science used to better the human lot and the rate at which, as a culture, we've exploited the wild; there's also a link between that vision and a more genuinely democratic human politics.

What then should I do? How to balance personal loyalty, ecological common sense, political realism, aesthetic inclination, cultural guilt, and leave room for the play of all those things I know I don't know enough about, possibilities I can't yet imagine? I don't know. If wilderness is not chaos, but complex, living pattern, it can, at least to some extent, be understood. But if it is complex, living pattern and not a dissociated array of raw materials, then that understanding will consist of more than a set of facts about the bottom line. Coming to it will be a bit like learning how to dance. It will require musicality, patience, social courage, attention to the other and, above all, time.

We might even say that the acquisition of such virtues — the coordinated wisdom of *agros* and *agrios* that we must allow the non-human to teach us — is what culture is about. But time is not a virtue. Time, as Anaximander suggested several centuries ago, is the judge of virtue, that which assesses the justice or injustice of all coming-to-be and passing-away. Time is what neither I nor the poplars, neither the farm nor the beavers, have on our side. In its absence, we must choose without discernment, and any principled action we might take will carry the taint of imposed, rather than responsive, order. In its absence we will fail to enact an agricultural relation even to the wilderness of our own lives.

[1]*River in a Dry Land: A Prairie Passage*, (Toronto: Stoddart Publishing, 2000). p. 142.

THE HEART OF THE WORLD
Yehuda Amichai

BARRY CALLAGHAN

Leprous, I sit among potsherds and nettles,
at the foot of a wall eaten by the sun.

— Rimbaud

JERUSALEM IS STONE WANTING TO BE WATER. Jerusalem is a dry wave at the centre of the earth: "When God created the world He placed the waters of the ocean around the earth. And in the heart of the inhabited world God placed Jerusalem . . . This is the heart of the world."

Jerusalem has a heart as crooked as ecclesiastical sheets, as crooked as yellow thorn branches, dry in their silence. In the alleyways there is no sound of water. By a wrought-iron window in a stone house on a rise called Yemin Moshe, looking across a gully to Jaffa Gate, Yehuda Amichai the poet sits hunched forward, solid and fleshy through the shoulders and his face is red from the sun. "And what about love?" I ask.

"It goes without saying," he says.

"It goes?"

"Sometimes it goes, sometimes it doesn't come."

He lives with his wife Hana in a stone house outside the city walls. She is smoking a pipe so small it fits in the palm of her hand. She has an open face, big eyes. In his eyes, there is a melancholy stillness as he says, "When you live in a house here, it's like living in the skins of all the men who've owned the house, maybe not friends, maybe enemies. It's very tiring to walk around naked in your own house wearing so many different skins." Desert winds pass over the house, the gravel hills and twisted olive trees and thorn bushes. The winds never soothe the city: it is too much a stone boat of bloodshed and benedictions, too weighed down to ever be soothed. To escape, prophets and holy men have always gone into the desert to be alone in the harsh light with their harsh desert god:

> And I'm like someone standing in
> the Judean desert, looking at a sign:
> "Sea Level."
> He cannot see the sea, but he knows.

Amichai and I sit in the cooling shadows and talk of Yeats and Ted Hughes, Lowell and Agnon, and we eat dates. "The place you are staying," he says, "Abu Tor . . . it means Father of the Ox. Named after an old man who lived there on that hill. Agnon has written a story about Abu Tor, but I forget it. There are too many stories here." As a poet, he has been forced to go to war and then limp back to his solitude, and then go and then come back, telling stories about war, smuggling arms from the Sinai desert, scouting in the Negev desert. "Poets are like foot soldiers, all by themselves out there. They get wounded." He is a man who thinks with a limp, the way Adam couldn't count his ribs without thinking of Eve. That's the way his mind works, analogically. He moves from the thing to the idea. He can't help himself.

The Real presence is the image. In his eye, it is the flesh that is made word, the Christian mystery of the Word made flesh put in reverse, leading not to death on a cross but to poetry as a rebuttal to death:

Like an infant messing itself with food
I want to mess myself with the world's problems.

All over my face, my eyebrows,

my shirt, my trousers, the tablecloth.

The dress of my love, my mother,

the mountains and the sky, all the people,
the feet of angels.

It was during the battle for Jerusalem that he said: " . . . everything is dry and there is no ocean of water, yet the Sea of Jerusalem is the most terrible sea of all." He walks the stone alleys of the old city like a sailor walks on board a ship. Even the postal contraction for Jerusalem on envelopes is D — (that is, Sea). Walking with him in the city I have seen the sea in the faces of men on their way to the Wailing Wall, men who believe they can sit in a stone boat and enter eternity.

"They think," Amichai says with an impish smile, "that Jerusalem is the Venice of God."

"In the beginning, God said — let there be light," he laughs, "but there was too much light. There is still too much light. We never get used to the hard light. We're forest people. We dream of the dark (*Every now and then someone says, even after forty or fifty years: 'The sun is killing me'*)". Shtetl Jews and forest Jews (like Amichai's people, farmers from Würzburg forests in southern Germany) dream of dark groves of trees, medieval cities, and Slavic knights turned to stone, covered with forest moss and forest streams running through the moss. So, too, the dream in the old city is of dark groves, of underground grottoes, of cooling dark vacancies, a dream of water. Always the absence of water. In Jerusalem, men want to be healed, to begin again, blessed by water. But men carry too much of the desert in their hearts. Men walk on stone believing it is water. It is a city of men. They fall and break their knees but somehow Amichai has not fallen:

> Every day I know the miracle of
> Jesus walking upon the waters,
> I walk through my life without drowning.

There is something dangerous on the air, like the taste of brass on the tongue.

The sun strafes everything in sight.

"People can lose their minds here," Amichai says, "you better be careful."

Yes.

Yes. Like his

> Rapists in deep slumber in the forest
> dreaming about real love.

He agrees that lots of people among the settlers lost their minds back before 1948, and that the seeds of their failure have been hidden in the hard soil. A kibbutznik from the Galilee, a man named Muki Tsur (the son, I believe, of the ambassador to Paris), has told me that the settlers back in the twenties kept public books in each kibbutz dining hall and every night the men and women wrote down their small joys, and a lot of pain . . . accusing each other and themselves of fear, cowardice, crimes, despair . . . and he said there were many suicides. The books were hidden away, which was a kind of betrayal, because fathers then told their sons protective lies, told them that the early years had been as green with hope as the sea as they stared into the desert with their backs turned to the sea.

"Times," Amichai says, "have taught us you can run bankrupt, but anyway you go on; you collapse, yet everything is normal. We are paying the price of pragmatic thinking. We have had to change our attitude so many times that by now the problems are empty. Our first feeling about the holocaust was revenge, but we are security-haunted. So whoever helps us to go on living physically is our friend, and so the Germans helped us and they are our friends. Again and again we have made such changes; it breaks you, makes you collapse, but in order not to break, you just put yourself into little pieces because it's much harder to break little pieces than to break one big piece." A little later I ask: "You and your friends, you're coming apart at the seams?" He laughs, his laughter always muffled. "Yes, yes. I think it is one of the deep feelings one has in this country. You can live with it. It even makes your life richer."

Walking slowly arm in arm we glide along the stones. The alley takes on a softness, a fluidity. "It's easy to create madness," he says, "if you take away memory from a man who is remembering . . . "

Everything is too close here, too intense, dream piled on dream. The holy men are the great pilers. They believe they possess the Navel of the World, an omphaloid stone that they say was measured by Christ's own hand, and they say that they've got the tomb of Adam, too, buried beneath Christ's gibbet, and they say that Adam was granted absolution because the divine blood shed on the gibbet fell on his bones, and they are sure that they've got the print of Adam's footbone in stone, and close by, the seven footprints of Abraham and Isaac, and they say that from exactly the same stone, Mohammed leapt off his horse into heaven, the hoofprint only a stone's throw from the grotto of Mary, who also leapt into heaven, her grotto close to another chamber where the blood of the crucified Christ stains a stone which was also the altar upon which Abraham offered Isaac before it became the altar on which Melchisedec offered . . . altars and blood . . . the great temple must have been a slophouse full of blood . . . bodies tangled and piled on each other:

> God's hand in the world
> like my mother's
> in the guts of a slaughtered hen . . .

There is no distance in Jerusalem. It is a walled city, melancholic, ecstatic. It holds heat during the day, it holds a chill at night, a snake cut in two, it goes on twisting. It is an ingrown city

> full of tired Jews
> Always whipped into memorial days and feasts
> Like bears dancing on aching legs.
> What does Jerusalem need? It doesn't need a mayor,
> It needs a ringmaster with a whip in his hand
> To tame prophecies and to train prophets to gallop
> Round and round in a circle . . .

"So much prophecy," he says, "so much sadness."

And he says he has seen sadness in the eyes of "*the Joint Chiefs of Staff consisting of Job, his friends, Satan, and God, around a small table.*" He, too, has sadness in his eyes:

> *My child still unborn is also a war orphan*
> *of three wars in which I was not killed,*
> *but he is a war orphan of all of them.*

It is 8:30 on a Thursday evening in the square that faces the Wall. The army is bulldozing Arab homes to open up more of the Wall. The Arabs are wailing. At the Wall the night before, brought there by an actress who knew Amichai, I had watched a swearing-in ceremony for paratroopers, the stride of the troopers (very British), the abrasive nasal harangue of the company commander over the loudspeakers, and then the burning of their "insignia" — letters on fire in the dark night sky, unsettling to the actress as it was to me, as if we were looking through the lens-eye of Leni Riefenstal.

"Anyway," she said defensively, "they are giving the Arabs better homes than they've ever had before."

"Right."

"No, it's wrong, but sometimes you have to do something wrong so that you can do what's right."

To do what is right by doing something wrong, to believe you are right while you know you are wrong, means learning how to forget, though

> *forgetting someone is like*
> *forgetting to put out the light in the back yard*
> *and leaving it on all day:*

it's this light, though,
that makes you remember.

Sons and fathers wrapped in fringed prayer shawls stand face to the Wall . . . that curious white-faced rocking of the men, a furtive pent-up sensuality in their bodies, pitching forward as if in pain, on the balls of their feet, tilting on their heels, like men trying to hold to the deck of a ship in a heavy sea.

I speak of this rocking to Amichai.

"Rocking soothes a baby," he says, "but it's the circumcision of the baby that does it to us. Pain. We never forget the pain. We live with the memory of pain all our lives."

Men among men, sharing the severed hood. It is their bond as they hunger for water. They know women are the water carriers but the covenant is sealed by blood, the knife. Women, the water carriers are unclean in their blood. It's a lot of confusion. So confusing men sometimes howl in their dreams and wake up sopping wet, their mouths dry.

I am wakened by the howling of dogs in the night, dogs down in the valley, and then I hear them howling during the day. Amichai tells me that there is a Canine Insane Asylum in the valley for dogs driven mad during the *khamsin*, a time of breath-eating heat and desert winds.

"This city," I tell him, feeling dread, "this city is like being trapped inside somebody's story that is all honey and bees and you get stung and you eat sweet and you get stung and you eat sweet, and it's perfect, it seems perfect because it's all of a piece, it rhymes, and I woke up the other night because I was freezing and I wanted out of here, but I not only didn't know how to get out, I forgot right away as soon as I warmed up that I wanted out . . . "

"You sound like someone crazy . . . "

"I sound like I gotta stop hanging around with you . . . "

We are tired from walking in the sun. When we get back to the house we will wash our

eyes with a lot of water
so as to see the world once more
through the wet and hurt.

Cats lie slumped in the roof gutters waiting for rain. Someone is playing an oboe. An old beard of brown grass hanging from a stone window ledge. A Chassid in his hot fur hat, wheeling an empty baby carriage down the stairs of the Dolorosa, says defiantly, touching a soldier with his long pale hand, that the Messiah will come only when there is springwater.

And it is said that the Sea of Ezekiel is under Jerusalem,
and that sea is sealed off. The Chassidim say they are the
waters of the Abyss; when the spring is discovered, then
the Messiah will come. Until that time of trembling,
Jerusalem is a sea of stone, a golden basin filled with scor-
pions.

In 326, the Emperor Constantine's mother, Helena, discovered a cistern close by a demolished temple to Venus, and in the cistern, the three crosses and the holy nails. The cross was true, she said, because of its power to raise the dead . . . a sign of the Messiah. A section of the cross was kept on the holy site; slivers were scattered among the empire's churches. The nails were forged into the bridle of Constantine's war horse, and set on his helmet.

He rode his horse into the world brandishing the cross.

Christ came to the city on a donkey, looking for his cross.

On Palm Sunday, the beginning of Holy Week, I walk out of a cypress grove close to the Garden of Gethsemane, the garden of the kiss, holding a small braided cross of palm. I am in a long procession of schoolgirls, black-robed and bearded priests, older women carrying umbrellas to shield themselves from the sun, with Jewish graves on the hillside and an army helicopter cracking the air open with its pulsing *thwack-thwack*, swoops over the valley of Hinom, where Abraham is said to lie in a tomb, and then swings out toward Jericho and the road to the Dead Sea, and then back across the vale of Gihon (where the builders of Baal placated their priests by impaling their firstborn):

> *The air above Jerusalem is saturated with prayers*
> *and dreams.*
> *Like the air above industrial towns*
> *It is hard to breathe.*

Again and again, the helicopter angles down toward us, clattering over the hillside seeded with sepulchres. At the Tomb of David — a great long stone box — the guide tells a group of Jews from Newark that the archeologists have an actual hair from David's beard; and close by, in another room, the walls are bricked as if they are ovens . . . a tidy *chambre* to commemorate the dead in the death camps . . . I cannot bring myself to tell the guide that the ovens in Auschwitz are fake, too, the reals ones were destroyed and then faux ovens were built, a protective lie, so that pilgrims would have something to look at in their need to be appalled . . .

The dead in the camps, David's whisker; the mind goes blank. The sun is white, the stones at the top of the walls are white, stones that once were sealed with molten lead, and what seems to be the shadow of a bird is only a dry yellow thorn bush. In the bend of a wall, the snout of a lion's-head fountain is stopped-up with cement.

"We, those of my generation," Amichai says, "believed that still, through politics, there was a way out, out of this entrapment. Your generation still believed a little bit. But your son, he has no interest in politics because he knows there is no way out."

Yet Amichai writes:

An Arab shepherd is seeking a kid
on Mount Zion,
And on the opposite hill I seek my little son.
An Arab shepherd and a Jewish father
Both in their temporary failure.
Our two voices meet above
The Sultan's Pool in the valley between . . .
Afterwards we found them between the bushes,

And our voices returned to us
And we wept and laughed deep inside ourselves.
Searches for a kid or for a son were always
The beginning of a new religion in these mountains.

Near the Ninth Station of the cross, a soldier sits in the gutter between roofs, overseeing at the strolling pilgrims. Two black-hatted Jews — Neturei Karta Chassids — ("the black crow people from Meah Sh'earim," as Amichai has called them,) hurrying white-faced along the alley, the wind flapping in their long black surcoats, do not look up at the soldier. They refuse to recognize the soldier. The Messiah, they say, has not come. The State is stillborn. They spit when the state is mentioned. They are true believers. In Meah Sh'earim, they have their signs: "The Nazis used our

bodies for soap, the Israelis use our bodies for money." No
wonder prophets saw scorpions inside wheels of fire in the
air and it is no wonder that men hungering for the sound
of water, as they head out into the desert to dream of the
sea, discover that the desert hills have the sensuous roll of
women's hips and thighs, and it is no wonder that they
dream of stuffing her

> *bed with apples*
> *(as it is written in the Song of Songs)*
> *so we'd roll smoothly*
> *on a red, apple-bearing bed.*

"Under the Dome of the Rock is a remarkable limestone,
it occupies, with its regular form, the greater part of the area
beneath; and is surrounded by a gilt iron railing, to keep it
from the touch of the numerous pilgrims. It appears to be
the natural surface of the rock of Mount Moriah . . . At the
southeast corner of this rock is an excavated chamber,
called by Mahomedans the Noble Cave, to which there is
a descent by a flight of stone steps. This chamber is irregular in form, and its superficial area is about six hundred
feet, the average height seven feet; it derives a peculiar
sanctity from having been, successively, (according to
Mahomedan tradition,) the praying-place of Abraham,
David, Solomon, and Jesus: its surface is quite plain, and
there are a few small altars. In the center of the rocky pavement is a circular slab of marble, which being struck, returns
a hollow sound, clearly showing that there is a well or exca-
vation beneath; this is called, by the Mahomedans, *Bir
arruah*, the well of souls — the well of wicked messengers
we must suppose, this being the narrow entrance to the
Mahomedan hell."

As for the well of messengers and their resurrection,

Afterward they'll get up
all at once, and with a sound of moving chairs
face the narrow exit.

And their clothes are wrinkled
and clods of soil and cigarette ash
are scattered over them
and fingers will uncover in an inside pocket
a theatre ticket from a long-gone season . . .

And their eyes are red from so much sleeplessness
underground.
And immediately — questions:
What time is it?
Where did you put mine?
When? When?

Good Friday. The day of The Wounds of Light. Crowds gather at St. Stephen's Gate under four stone lions, men and women shoulder large dark brown varnished crosses and begin a slow, stumbling processional along the Way of Sorrows, stopping first at a broad courtyard, The Place of Judgement — and there, in the polished, almost translucent paving stones, are a carved star, a carved sword, a spiked crown with the letter B, a scorpion . . . the games, we are told, played by bored soldiers, incising their signs in stone . . . except, this is not the place of the Judgement Hall. This is a section of Hadrian's forum where the "guardrooms" were actually shops; and across the Dolorosa is the Church of the Flagellation and the Place of Condemnation and they say that this is where Christ received his cross . . . except he did not shoulder it here, not in this Roman temple yard. Still, the crowd moves on through the cobbled alleyways of the market, past tray upon tray of Arab sweets soaked in honey, and leather purses, meats, worry beads, the crowd chanting prayers, lunging forward, led by brown-robed Franciscans, and I let the foot of their huge cross rest on my shoulder, for this ritual has become a devotional Way of Sorrows in my mind, too . . . a pilgrimage toward death and resurrection because the truth is in the story not in the details . . . stopping where Christ was helped by Simon the Cyrene, where Veronica wiped his face, where he fell, and fell again, and fell for the third time at the Ninth Station where the best baklava in the old city is sold not far from where Amichai shops for vegetables and little Palestinian schoolgirls in maroon dresses sing in Armenian as the cross is twirled like a huge propeller, bruising my neck. This is done so that it will fit through a narrow passage into the sepulchre forecourt, the crowd bulging and surging toward the tomb within the church, a shabby little roundhouse tomb with a litter of paper currency and coins on the stone slab scooped up by a bearded priest, eyes drowsy with a dulled sensuality, dulled by too much candle smoke in the cramped, sweaty chamber. I want air and spin out of the tomb, past women wrapped in black and a blind man whose eyes are bleached white, an old dream of apocalypse in his eyes, and outside, up on Olivet Hill, close to where Christ spoke to the apostles of the Last Things, there is the Church of Dominus Flevit, "The Lord Wept".

The church is shaped as a tear.

"The wine did not end," Amichai says, "but the eyes ran out of tears."

He has his father's eyes and his mother's graying hair on his head, as he makes his way home with his vegetables to sit

in a house that belonged to an Arab
who bought it from an Englishman
who took it from a German
who hewed it from the stones
of Jerusalem, my city:
I look upon God's world of others
who received it from others.
I am composed of many things
I have been collected many times
I am constructed of spare parts
of decomposing materials
of disintegrating words. And already
in the middle of my life, I begin,
gradually, to return them,
for I wish to be a decent and orderly person
when I'm asked at the border, "Have you anything
        to declare?"

"What I've got to declare is what I talk about over and over. Maybe I am a little boring, but my story of me sits at the middle, and everything around it—— like a sleepless lover who has cigarette butts on the floor all around his bed — are interpretations, different versions, *midrashim*, some foolish, some sad, it's how my life goes on, it's what I have to declare."

The beggars at Dung Gate listen as a scornful sabra declares,
    "God doesn't love us, and neither does the world. Too bad. It's no longer our problem, but their's. From now on,

they will not count in our calculations. We shall ignore them . . . I don't give a damn anymore whether humanity has a conscience or not. It never had any, that's what I think. I think all the grandiloquent talk about humanity's soul and conscience was invented by persecuted Jews as a shield or alibi. So they wouldn't have to fight . . . Many persecuted Jews let themselves be massacred. They should have risen up in fury, they should have revolted."

"Bounce the ball. Bounce."

"Hup, one two three four . . . "

"Shoot . . . "

"Hup, one two three four . . . "

We are on a patio surrounded by bushes on a terraced slope outside the old city, the home of a painter. The patio backs on to a house wall. There's a German Shepherd sitting under a round table (is it just me? why do I find it strange to see more and more Jews who own German Shepherds?) and five or six red kitchen chairs and a netless basketball hoop up on the wall. Hana and Amichai's old friend, Dennis Silk, are at the table. There's wine and water. She's smoking her pipe.

I am bouncing a basketball, firing it up at the hoop. Amichai, in jeans and a loose shirt, is marching with mock military sterness, carrying a rod like a rifle over his shoulder.

"Shoo . . . shoot . . . "

bump bump bump,

dribbling the ball on stone paving.

"The last war," he says, "they put me in charge of the Mount of Olives, in a hotel. I had an office. And my men brought in a man who wouldn't obey the curfew, and I said, I know you from somewhere, and he said he was Burt Lancaster, he was playing Moses or somebody who I knew, so I was a big military man in the war in charge of Moses on the Mount of Olives."

bump,

"Shoot."

He is still marching back and forth.

Everyone is laughing. Hana says, "He is trying to take Amichai hill," puffing on her pipe.

"Which hill is that?" I ask.

"It's a hill where women go to restore their virginity," he says, a mischievous light in his eyes.

"Opposite Mount Zion," Hana says.

"A crop of rock . . . the women crouch on their haunches over the stone at night, flapping their bent arms like wings."

The ball caroms off the side of the rim and rolls away. Amichai stops marching and sits down, holding his side as if he were counting his ribs. There are sandwiches, salad in styrofoam boxes. And bottles of water.

"I'll tell you how things have changed," he says. "The poor, the impoverished, no longer turn to the left. Here, they are right wing . . . no one will deal with what has to be done here?"

"Meantime, we can do nothing," Hana says.

"Pray," I say, laughing.

(But he is capable of a deeper sardonic laughter, because — as he has written — there are Hebrew prayers for everything, even prayers that are said after defecating, a prayer thanking God for having created man with orifices, a prayer to God, knowing full well that

He who created man
and filled him full of holes

will do the same to soldiers
afterwards, in war.)

After lunch, as we are leaving the patio, I hand him his soldiering rod, his rifle, but he hunches forward and taps the stone walk, turning the rod into a cane. "Me, already, I'm an old man," he says.

"You're not old, you're middle-aged. My father is in old age, he has three girlfriends in their thirties, who take him to supper, and the proof that he is in his old age is that his real pleasure is that they pay the bill."

Amichai laughs as loud as I've ever heard him laugh.

"This is a father who is not bored," he asks, "he doesn't look back?"

"No, never. Hardly ever."

"I knew an old couple," he says conspiratorially, "so they concentrated on their beginning, how they began, telling each other the same old story over and over until they were so bored that they badgered and badgered each other all day about how happy they were."

He tosses the rod into the bushes.

"There has been this rumor about God," he says, "that He has gone missing. Several men said this, Theodor Adorno said this, that after Auschwitz it was no longer possible to talk about God. But anyway we started talking about God again,"

like a child that still uses the
Baby talk of its first years,
And still can't say
God's real name but says *Elokim, Hashem, Adonai,*
Dada, Gaga, Yaya, *for ever and ever, sweet distortions.*

And Amichai asks:

My God, my god, why? Have you forsaken me?
My God, my god. Even then you had to call him
twice.
The second time already a question, a first doubt: my
God?

At Easter, in 1697, Henry Maundrell wrote: "Thus, if you would see the place where St. Anne was delivered of the Blessed Virgin, you are carried to a Grotto; if the place where the Blessed Virgin selected Elizabeth, if that of the Baptist's . . . if that of the Agony, or that of St. Peter's Repentance, or that where the Apostles made the creed . . . all these places are also Grottoes. And in a word, wherever you go, you find almost everything is represented as done underground . . . "

Skulls are underground.

The small hill where Christ was crucified was called Golgotha, Skull Hill.

Skull Hill is now buried within the walls of the Church of the Holy Sepulchre and Herman Melville, the old pilgrim sailor, haunted by Ahab and the leprous white whale, came to the Holy Sepulchre in 1857: "Ruined dome — confused and half-ruinous pile. Labyrinths and terraces of mouldy grottoes, tombs, and shrines. Smells like a dead-house, dingy light. At the entrance, in a sort of grotto in the wall, a divan for Turkish policemen, where they sit cross-legged and smoking, scornfully observing the continuous troop of pilgrims entering and prostrating themselves before the anointing-stone of Christ, which veined streaks of a mouldy red looks like a butcher's slab. Nearby is a blind stair of worn marble ascending to the reputed Calvary . . . and the hole in which the cross was fixed and through a narrow grating as over a cole-cellar, the rent in the rock!"

Outside of the Sepulchre, Amichai, in a moss-brown suit jacket, all three buttons buttoned, self-enclosed, puts his hand to his eyes, a shielding hand:

Many a sailor has seen a cross on the water.
A cross of blood.
A sign.
To be made in blood.

After supper in his house with Hana and their boy and girl, he walks me halfway to Abu Tor and startles me as we go down stone stairs in the dark. He asks a question no writer has ever asked me. "Do you believe Jesus was the messiah?"

"He was like everything else in this city," I say, "nothing is what it seems."

"Yes?"

"The messiah was supposed to be from the line of David, that's what they said, and David was Joseph's house, except Jesus wasn't Joseph's son, his father was a bird who whispered into his mother Mary's ear. That's why seventeenth-century puritans, who covered their women from chin to toe, thought ears are so sexy."

On July 15, 1099, Fulcher de Chartres, a Crusader, came clanking across a stone courtyard in Jerusalem wearing his iron suit, looking for the Holy Sepulchre, and he wrote: "With drawn swords, our people ran through the city; nor did they spare anyone, not even those pleading for mercy. The crowd was struck to the ground, just as rotten fruit falls from shaken branches, and across from windblown oak . . . On top of Solomon's Temple, to which they had climbed in fleeing, many were shot to death with arrows and cast down headlong from the roof. Within the Temple about ten thousand were beheaded. If you had been there, your feet would have been stained up to the ankles with the blood of the slain . . . it was an extraordinary thing to see our squires and poorer people split the bellies of those dead Saracens, so that they might pick out the besants from their intestines, which they had swallowed down their horrible gullets while alive. After several days, they made a great heap of their bodies and burned them to ashes, and in these ashes they found the gold more easily . . . It was pleasing to God at that time, that a small piece of the Lord's Cross was found in a hidden place. From ancient times until now it had been concealed by religious men, and now, God willing, it was revealed by a certain Syrian. He, with his father as conspirator, had carefully concealed and guarded it there. This particle, reshaped in the style of the cross and artistically decorated with gold and silver, was first carried to the Lord's Sepulchre and then to the Temple joyfully, with singing and giving thanks to God, who for so many days had preserved this treasure, His own and ours."

A patrimony reclaimed. A city reclaimed every hour:

The city plays hide-and-seek

among her names:
Yerushalayim, al-Quds, Salem, Jeru, Yeru, all the while

Whispering her first, Jebusite name: U'vus,
Y'vus, Y'vus, in the dark. She weeps
with longing: Aelia Capitolina, Aelie, Aelia.
She comes to any man who calls her
at night . . .

There is a great cave that echoes under the city. It is dry at the mouth and made of liquid stone along the roof and in this vacant darkness, musk reeking womb of the city, women have what Amichai calls "the waterfall of words within." This is where a woman

> *at night is naked and alone.*
> *And sometimes she's naked and not alone.*

This is where

> *You can hear the sound of bare feet*
> *running away: and it was death.*
>
> *And afterwards the sound of a kiss*
> *like the fluttering of a moth*
> *caught between two panes of glass.*

Though the stones of the city are celibate, Amichai warns a woman who appears "oiled with suntan oil as if on a beach" that pale bachelors, lechers, are lying in wait for her in the alleys, and

> *the groaning trousers*
> *of old men, too, their unholy lust in the guise of prayer*
> *and grief*

but he is not one of them. He is not without his own yearning, even lust, but as he wonders about sexuality his lust quits him —

> *What's it like to be a woman?*
> *What's it like to feel*
> *vacancy between legs and curiosity*
> *under the skirt, in summer, in wind,*

and chutzpa at the haunches?

What's it like to have a whole voice,
that never broke?
To dress and undress slitherly
slinkily caressively
like wearing olive oil,
to anoint the body with lithe fabrics,
a silky something,
a murmuring nothing of peach or mauve?
A male dresses with crude gestures of
buckling and edgy undoing,
angles, bones and stabs in the air,
and the wind's entangled in his eyebrows.

What's it like to "feel a woman"?
And your body dreams you.
What's it like to love me?

Amichai every morning wakes and watches the sea retreat from his face and he sees in the mirror not an exhausted lover but "the floor of the sea: dry with cracks and rocks and savage winds." He says he grew up like that with memories of the soft green sea still on his face and anchors from abandoned ships hung as house decorations, as

> *our hearts too*
> *will be just an amulet,*
> *hung inside in dreams and blood.*

In the Holy Sepulchre crowds are waiting for the first sign of the Resurrection of the shed of blood. There are two small windows in the tomb and fire bursts out of the windows . . . hand-held candles snatch the flame . . . Little has changed since Claude Reignier Conder wrote in the 1870s: "Torches were passed out of the fire-hole, and the fire spread over the church, as the roar grew louder and louder. The flame spread, seeming to roll over the whole crowd, till the church was a sea of fire, which extended over the roof to the chapel, and ran up the galleries and along the choir. Meantime a dreadful bell was clanging away . . . A dense blue fog, made by the smoke, and a smell of burning wax rose up, and above all, a quiet gleam of light shone down from the roof."

Black Abyssinian monks who live on the roof, who live a contemplative village life in small plastered hutches and cells built on top of the sepulchre, have come out of their crow's nests and are down in the square parading under a large multicoloured tent to the beat of small drums. Their bishop, in a glittering robe, carries a jewelled umbrella. Boys in white *jalibayas* leap around him . . . They are hunting as they do every year for the body of Christ as the sun goes down.

"Everybody," Amichai says, "is a sailor in Jerusalem without knowing it, sailors or passengers, mechanics or captains, everyone according to the pattern of his life or character." And among them, a man Amichai knows who has covered up the concentration camp numbers on his arm with a tattoo, the blue scales and tail of a mermaid . . . covering the numbers so he can forget the past, all the fathers dead, but not covering the numbers completely so that he will remember the past, the fathers dead . . .

When the moon is full,
it will be my father's memorial day.
It's always so.

The day of his death will never fall
in summer or in spring.

I put little stones on his tomb:
a sign I was here,
the calling card of one alive
on the big stone of my father. My father,
causer and affected,
your alarm clock breaks my body.

Two sabbath candles of my mother
travel gently side by side on the streets,
towed by a ship, not seen . . .

Father, I now like to wash and comb my hair.
Aside from this, I haven't changed.

The scant information on your tombstone
is less than a passport.

There's no police to tell
I'm a murderer.
When I get home I'll lie down,
arms spread as if crucified.

It calms me, Father.

All the bells ring on Easter Sunday. The sun shines and all the bells ring. The dead body has not been found by the Abyssinians. "Somewhere out there is Shiloh . . ."

In a sepulchre chapel, squat women in black dresses and black shawls crowd onto the altar, bullying one another, shoving and squirming, stubborn in their joy, pitiless in their grasp of it, as they let out a joyous shout tinged by pain . . .

The sound of stone becoming water. Soldiers stand on the roofs, cradling their guns.

Amichai, done with his shopping, has all the vegetables he needs for his family. There are tourists crowded into the arab alleys, tourists who have bought filigreed arab jewellery and they have put on grave faces at the Wailing Wall and they have had their pictures taken among the famous dead at Rachel's Tomb and Herzl's Tomb and on top of Ammunition Hill, making — as Amichai says — visits of condolence before heading to their air-conditioned hotels, just as he is heading home to his stone house in Yemin Moshe.

"Once," he says, "I sat on the steps by a gate at David's Tower, I placed my two heavy baskets at my side. A group of tourists was standing around their guide and I became a target marker. 'You see that man with the baskets? Just right of his head there's an arch from the Roman period. Just right of his head.' But he's moving, he's moving — I said to myself, redemption will come only if they're told: you see that arch from the Roman period? It's not important: but next to it, left a little and down a bit, there sits a man who's bought fruit and vegetables for his family."

DANCING OUTDOORS

DAVIDA MONK

AT FIRST I AM AWARE OF THE DIMENSIONS OF SPACE at the
mouth of the coulee. The space is the negative of the
coulee's form. The coulee's sides rise directly from where I
stand, then billow, cave and overlap their way into the
distance. Contained within the shaped space is the sculpted
palette of sound. The sound of my breathing, intimate and
inside, my steps on the path, close and underneath me, two
ducks lifting off the creek in the near distance, a truck
beeping at the gravel pit a couple miles away. These sounds
place themselves relative to my location in articulate strata
and precise orientation. Their textures relieve an underlying hum which is the sound of my ears getting used to the
relative silence.

The density of sound and silence calls forth the recognition of other densities. The path I walk on is pounded
firm from cattle while the prairie turf on either side of the
path yields softly, crunchily. The moment itself is dense
with information, the visual field of fractals, the tactile
impressions of the tips of grass and brush without, and the
layers of memory, anticipation, and desire within. Each
breath I draw is flavoured and cooled by the faint vegetal

pungency of this late autumn. A dry season eclipsing a dry summer, a dry spring and winter. The air moves its coolness around me. Particularly at the back of my neck and my calves. I recognize that I have not dressed as warmly as I should have.

I sense the moving stillness of life through a continuousness form, the coulee and its flora. The rootedness and self containment of every hillside, bush, sprig of grass and lichened rock encouraging the same presence in me. Presence. If I am moved now to dance it is through self-conscious desire, searching. Somehow I know that it is more important now to receive, to be and not to do.

As I walk deeper into the mouth of the coulee, its sides wrap around in protection, and I feel how the earth calls up association and memory in me. I react to what I see with the most basic of conversations. Call and response. This mimetic impulse establishes relationship through a physical sympathy which is consistent with the play that is part of dancing outdoors. It is an impulse to direct interpretation, both inevitable and embraceable. I find that if I don't embrace it I will have to constantly put it aside because it is so insistent.

Perversely though, in mimetic activity the critical mind yearns to censure and thereby block discovery that might emerge from these moments that are in fact honest beginnings of relationship.

The body answers the gnarled brush with contortions of its own. The head bobs heavily on the spine beside the tall grass that bears the weight of snow. The mimetic desire that spurs me to imitate shape allows for discovery of what is beyond shape. As when the fingers reaching to express the spirit of the branching tips of the saskatoon bush inexplicably transmute into song. I sing a song that seems to come from the place where the bush is rooted. I follow the song and let it come, let it make me feel like a child. A similar desire also leads to the internalization of a visual pattern and results in a rhythm articulated the length of the spine. The shoulder blades and elbows trace, repeat, diminish and embellish the folding lines of receding hills. Mimetic impulse can sometimes turn around inside itself and become a reaction to the source of inspiration. I find that the response that comes to a rugged and jagged rock cairn is the willowing of the arms. Response leads me away from the mimetic and towards a number of options, each one evolving to its own particularity.

In contemporary dance, works are made in studio space and presented in theatre space. The dance environment is always a space. The way dance space is characterized can determine the way the body moves. The dance can express itself in internal, near, far or infinite space. It can be more or less dense, and produce movement qualities of resistance and fluidity. Space is engaged by the dancer's imagination and summoned into an exchange in a way that supports movement and groundedness while it hones the sense of direction. A particular space is shaped by what it contains. Its textures influence a dancer's use of time and rhythm. Understanding the importance of space is a fundamental key to appreciating the expressive motive and language of the dance. The sensuous experience is that movement enacts space. Space is the energetic canvas for motion. There is no dance without space.

I first felt the thrill of limitless space in 1988 on a trip to the Cypress Hills of southwest Saskatchewan. At a chance roadside stop, I stepped out of the vehicle and my body loosed a surprising spontaneous dance. Naively apprehending the landscape I rode the body's delight as I twirled and spun in the centre of a 360-degree world. The dance came freely, without forethought, and in the manner of any true gift, it moved me to deep gratitude. Ever since then as part of my practice I have been dancing outdoors, following the mystery of that moment, proposing responses through my creation and performance.

The senses are the medium of exchange between the dancer and her environment. The dancer works to develop and refine sensory experience in order to expand the range of choices available to her physical expression. There are the general senses of touch, pressure, vibration, cold, heat, and pain, and the primary senses with their specialized receptors of vision, hearing, smell and taste. All of these work with the sense of proprioception which tells us where and how our bodies are in space. The senses combine to create body awareness, the most visceral experience of self.

As powerful and necessary as the senses are, the dancer cannot simply accept them. To attain a state of heightened receptivity with the environment the dancer has to reorganize the conventional hierarchy of perception. One learns quickly that eyesight does not simply transmit visual information. The unexamined visual sense is a projection of the unexamined state of mind. In our culture it carries with it the trap of sceneryization, the naming game phenomenon that objectifies and converts a real world into language, scientific studies or postcard images. I use the eyes guardedly, always with attention, aware of their potential treachery.

Whatever is said of focus can be said of the mind. Naturally the eyes roam freely and instruct us on the nature of the roaming mind. The conscious use of the eyes brings us to the conscious use of mental focus. Eyes-closed explorations in movement are necessarily limited spacially but not sensuously as hands, and sometimes other parts of the body can replace the eyes to surprising results. I was walking the deer path on the east slopes of a coulee and was drawn to a growth of saskatoons whose form suggested a dance of lingering exploration under its cloistered arches. I closed my eyes and extended my hands to better sense the character of the space. As my hands traveled and grasped the length of the stalks I sank to a crouch or rose to the balls of my feet, pulling away and leaning in, supporting the tortions of the body with the strength of my arms and the rootedness of the saskatoon bush. My shoulders, waist, hips and ribcage all explored the limits of movement within this space. The dance defined itself through what could be expressed within these limitations.

A diffuse focus, one that is soft, indirect and peripheral, takes advantage of some normally unexplored attributes of sight. Diffuse focus establishes itself naturally as we listen. It sensitizes us in a subliminal way to the weight and thickness of our bodies as part of the mass of all existence. It has a way of taking in the whole with its sense of sweep encouraging the perception of forms, and the smaller repeating patterns within larger forms. In that totality it picks up areas of focal interest which are of dramatic and formal potential in that they seem to express fundamental patterns echoed on many levels in the natural world and in our own lives. My sense is that these places draw us to them by their familiarity, by what they have to reveal about the condition of material and sensuous existence.

As the practice of diffuse focus draws us to the perception of the world it draws us away from the differentiated self. When we send our attention and focus to the periphery of perception our own personal periphery dissipates, creating the impression of an existential porousness that enhances the experience of exchange. We discover new sensations that belie the illusion of our separateness from the world. It is in this state that I question what is inside and what is outside myself. When I no longer know this, or anything else for sure, I have become open and receptive. In this state I live with flow, ambiguity and surprise.

Yet the eyes can be used analytically. No matter how closely I look at a leaf I will never succeed at making this experience a purely visual one. In the same way that a word or a phrase repeated over and over can reveal new meanings through sound, visual scrutiny meets up with the inspirited aspects of growth, the essence of being in each thing. Vision can take us from what can be seen to the recognition of life expressed through visible form, then even to our own deeper responses. It is through vision, assisted by cultivated intuitive apprehension, that the irregular variations of natural form can find their way directly or transformed into movement explorations.

Even the way eyes locate us in space deserves renewed appreciation. As we walk through the land visual perspectives change with our progress and offer a continuous reorganization of the elements in the visual field. Curving or rotating the spine at any point changes perspective, bending the knees changes perspective. We are used to this automatic accommodation and therefore not conscious of its impact on ourselves. The constant shifting does not feel discontinuous because our experience of the present moment is not defined by the visual sense alone.

Listening is different. Sound intrudes as powerfully on our personal space as does touch. We are affected immediately and deeply. To listen is to pay attention. Listening is a form of connection, a tuning of self to other. Listening serves not just as a metaphor for attention but as a sensory access to a multifaceted present-moment awareness. The listener moves simultaneously into the land of the imagination. In dance and in theatre the act of listening brings authentic presence to the performer as no other action can.

Simply walking the ground and heeding the irregularities of the surface with the pliability of the feet, ankles, knees and hips translates emanations through the spine. The more pliable and responsive the body the more full the physical and related experiences making for a continuous ride of subtlety and detail. The entire form of the body negotiates the unevenness as it travels, like a surfer negotiating a wave. Undulations, imbalances, trips and twists, even the anticipatory stretching of the hands. These are some of the body's responses to travelling across an irregular surface. It is a dance of balance fed by the rhythm of a two-beat walk in the space of the unknown.

If the dance is expressed on horseback, then the underlying rhythms vary between the two-beat trot, the three-beat canter and the four-beat walk. The particularities of the ground are translated through four legs and a horizontal spine, then to the rider's pelvis and vertical spine. That the motion is generated by another creature and translated through the human rider is an added excitement. I remember long mornings riding the prairie on a friend's ranch during calving season. When I lay down after lunch for a nap the motion continued. The body felt like a container of memories' fluids waving and crashing against each other, playing by heart the music of the landscape, creating their own music.

My dance response to the natural world is triggered by obstacles. Obstacles become elements of structure that characterize the improvisations and guide the choices I make. The same improvisational structure generates different dances depending on my own state of receptivity. As in any improvisation, the richness of discovery is promised only if I stay with an approach long after my first impulse to leave it. This is when the process shifts from mimetic and interpretive to responsive and intuitive. In this happy state the critical mind ceases interfering. The dance expresses a moment of transcendence dependent on this particular time and space.

In the grassy belly of the coulee lie a haphazard dispersal of partially embedded lichened rocks. They are sizeable, like pumpernickel bread. Some like coconuts. The rhythm of the dance that expresses itself among the rocks is free but the space is defined and the body's form is influenced by the rocky texture and spacial barrier. When the rocks are no longer elements of territorial definition but rather points of avoidance, a dance of changing directions results expressing a convoluted confusion. In the same space a sustained dance addresses the rocks as points of arrival and balance, places of desirable atonement and listening.

Up and down the sides of the coulee I dance the struggles and exhilarations of the hill. Each improvisation expresses the fact of the incline, with or against, and a particular physical response. Climbing is difficult, thickens the space, slows the pace. Descending is giddy, or cautious, and calls up associated memories. I remember how as a little girl I watched in horror as my grandmother tried desperately to climb up the down escalator in an effort to save me where I stood at the top, unable to enter the rhythm of the moving steps.

I wonder if the movement and musicality that come during these experiences reflect or block the essence of the obstacle, the incline, the space? Do they ever express the spirit of place? Dance outdoors, like any other expressive activity, often involves searching, being active and self conscious. My improvisations begin with curiosity, playfulness and trust, and they resolve or simply peter out. Often there are emotions of gratitude, intimacy and even love. At times it feels overstimulating. The professional concern of how I might make use of this experience, how I could apply it to dance-making seems completely beside the point. Dance, like any language, sometimes just gets in the way. I feel that the deepest nourishing connection I seek is distinct from but related to my artistic practice. I feel that it is not through the dance of action but through the dance of being. Stillness.

Most of what I do outside can't be transported to the theatre stage. If the improvisations are true to the space, to the whole environment, then they make no sense in the theatre. The moments of connection inspired by the environment are precious and as such permit no capture, no reenactment. But I am driven to acknowledge and express some measure of transference in my dances. At issue for me is how this transference can occur without interpreting and trivializing the natural world. I sense the most immediate aspect of the solution in my own body.

Outdoor dancing enlivens the dancer and widens her range of expression in a way that studio explorations do not do quite so readily. Basically, the responses that are required outdoors emphasize sensuous and integral experience as opposed to formal demonstration. The air, the light, the ground all make meaningful exchanges with the dancing body. On many levels it is a healthy pursuit. The dancer is impelled to let go of trends and appearances. Outdoors, if the dancer is listening, she cannot help but make enormous forays into her capacities of trust and intuition. The mind participates in the dance in a way that empowers the artist. The force of nature with which the dancer collaborates, and which she also finds within herself, is accepting of any movement choice. Outdoors, I learn to do what comes, no matter how inadequate it might feel. It is not what is danced outside but how dancing happens outside. The giving over to the experience of moving in the natural world serves to increase a dancer's artistry. The experience grants expressive freedoms. It tenderly insinuates the values of self-acceptance, humility, attention and intuition into practice.

Something else happens outdoors which is wonderfully mysterious. Sometimes I glimpse my connection to the greater ongoing creation. My periphery loses its definition, my flesh loses density and I dance in a strangely familiar vision of spacial freedom and divine light. My head pierces the sky. I feel of moisture. Desiccated and insubstantial I diffuse to contain the world, the world blooms spirit-like within me. I taste the fullness of the moment. I might be alone on a plain, among the hoodoos of Drumheller, in the tall grasses along the Bow River, or in the clay pits of the Whitemud Valley. Dancing outdoors is conversing with the trees in the deep coulees, and with the deer poised at a curious distance. It is transformative. I declare myself to the sky from a dried slough bed; I flash in the sunshine and I am the rain.

Landscapes like the Cypress Hills of southwest Saskatchewan, or the coulee near my home in Alberta, lend themselves beautifully to the situation and presentation of dance. There is however the practical problem of bringing an audience to the performance site.

In an attempt to address this problem I created a thirteen-minute landscape dance video, titled "Coulee", which features a sequence of movement scenes shot from particular perspectives within the coulee. My choreographic choices range from phrases related to my formal tradition that express an element of physical risk in the outdoor environment, to movement that responds to the space, to simple states of being. In this work I encounter the opposite of the problem of bringing outdoor dancing to the stage. Here in the middle of the natural world is artifice and technique. Hmmm. This doesn't seem right.

So what is the role of technique in the natural environment? Elements of vocabulary associated with my dance class are out of place. And yet isn't that often the case with western industrial culture and the natural environment? I live in a land with an ancient history of dance. When I undertake my outdoor dancing I am aware of this history and of my own very different one. Bringing my culture to the task of outdoor dance performance places the work in stark relief. And while this is not a misrepresentation of the truth, it falls short of artistic satisfaction. Of course the best use of technique is transparent and never synonymous with nor absent from expression. Technique means how. Interestingly, on the level of personal experience the techniques that form my studio practice tune me into the natural environment in a powerful way because they tune me into my animal body. As I enter the coulee I am aware that while threads of other business hang on, the body is enlivened to the present by my physical warm-up. In this state the lag of mind is hardly disconcerting. In fact the present awareness that my body achieves literally overcomes distractions and brings the mind easily to the moment. It is a big step, though, from physical preparedness to artistic product.

If I am to create dance works that are in greater sympathy with the environment, this might suggest the necessity of a completely new movement language. What can I hope to express? If it is complete at-one-ness that will satisfy then there is no need for performance at all, or artifice, or audience, just being. If what is to be expressed is the experience itself, sensitized by openness, candour and craft, then I must learn to dig deeper. For now the one thing that does feel correct is trust. I trust the urge to dance outdoors, and I accept the challenge of discovering and expressing the mysteries of this trust. I wonder if the extension of trust is like listening, and like touching, in that the effect is immediate and intimate. In fact it seems like the act of listening actually prompts the trust.

It could be that trusting my fascination with universal harmonies of form, pattern and motion prompted the first and enduring underpinnings of a recent creation process. The spiraling forces expressed in the Milky Way, the Coriolis Effect, cyclones, whirlpools and the Golden Section of the ancient Greeks are also expressed in and by the moving body. The study of spiral then brought me to an exploration of spiral traces around the body. This exploration organized itself in self similar repetitions of progressively finer scales, the kind of fractal expression of form found everywhere in the natural world. I discovered that exploring the body's spiraling potential generates new movement vocabulary as it bridges culture and nature.

During the same creation process I asked the dancers to bring in articles of personal value from which we would begin some new work, hoping to evolve dance ideas from connection. The next day one dancer brought into the studio a lichened rock that she had found in the Cypress Hills. Unbeknownst to her I had a collection of similar Cypress Hills treasures at home. The power of this influence triggered sections of dance expressing the interrelationships between creation, intuition and discovery in the natural world.

Everything, including the need for artistic acclaim, changes with trust. Trust allows the leaps of intuition, launches accelerated departures into new material, bestows direct ways of knowing. Perception breaks open and the illusion of separateness is flushed away in the draft. The inside and outside of existence are not only in exchange they are in sympathy, and the mind comes to know itself in its natural surroundings.

COCKS

PRUDENCE GRIEVE
i.m. A.R.

THE OLD HOUSE WAS OUT AT ALL ANGLES. It was wild.

If you dropped a pencil, it would roll off in any of three directions till it reached a wall or sneaked out under a door to the hall or the landing.

The floors had been tilting for years, I suppose. The tops of the doors had been shaved to keep pace with their lintels, and when you lay on the living-room couch the conflicting angles ganged up on you. The door frames and panels and baseboards, all askew with the windows and quarreling with each other, till you had to close your eyes or go funnelling down the rabbit hole.

But the house took us in. With its comfortable ghosts, and its old brick Ontario architecture. With its smell, once we'd exorcised the last tenants. With the nighttime chorus of creaks and retorts as it settled to sleep around us.

The huge old kitchen too, the pressed-tin ceiling and the McLaren wood cookstove beside the electric appliances. Where the sun came in in the morning, and where we ate and talked together. Whenever I was alone there I found myself singing.

I leaned on the sink and looked out across the yard at the great barn and the twenty-three acres of pasture sloping down to the woodlot.

Our inheritance.

On our third day there we watched Leni climb into the school bus, as blithe as I was fearful, and cleaned out some more of the basement, and then took our lunch up into the haymow above the barn.

"The light," I said. "Oh, the light." I could never have dreamed such a space. It seemed built to hold light, filled up from the open hatch high in the north wall: its pale skin of vertical planks, its long beams hewn from the giant pines whose absence haunted our woodlot, the roof arching thirty feet over us.

We lay on the bales of old hay, dwarfed by that airy architecture. Breathing the outside inside, the weather of barns. All that work and failure, all those seasons and history to make this playhouse for us. "It's a medieval hall," I said, and Aidan said, "Lie back and look up," and then it was the hold of *The Mayflower*, of *The Golden Hinde*, of *The Dawntreader*. He had me believing I might tumble down into those ribs. The open timbers, the broadaxe signatures, the mortise clefts wide as bibles. How high they dreamed when the trees on the hill were high, those carpenters sleeping under their Gaelic epitaphs, in the Holyrood graveyard.

There were pigeons down there at the keel of the ship, up there on the ridge pole; their amorous drone was the voice of the place. Leaning up again on my elbow, I could see swallows through the hatchway, in lines on the wires, facing south. Soon they'd leave, but their nests, and the scabs of old nests, were everywhere under the beams. Then the black cats came out to watch us. Wild shadows who lived on rats and sparrows, and made tunnels among the bales, and whose breath rasped like canvas. There'd be kestrel chicks, too, on a strut in the granary, and raccoons, and secret clutches of game hen's eggs in the bales — but that was the future.

The haymow's scent entered into me, never to leave. Making love in that space was the christening, while below came the cackle of triumph, or relief — or, it seemed to me, mockery — from an egg-proud hen, and then Oscar down in the yard, taking all of the credit, sounding the call to the rest of his harem.

Oscar. The first to meet us, the first to be named.

There's a young girl doing a dance in the slow Ontario rain, while her mother and the man who might become her father unload their belongings from the van parked up by the house. Can you call it a dance? She has never lived in the country, and here is this building, twice as long as the house, twice as high, with a side door open to the smells and the shadows and dim lights within, and this creature barring the way. He stands no higher than her thigh but he fills up the doorway. His head is huge and golden, but his face is as small as a doll's. A narrow hooked nose and mouth, with an orange eye that will not leave hers, wicked and mocking. His legs shift when hers do, his head cocks over and watches her. His moustaches and eyebrows quiver; they are pink, wrinkled jellies.

The great, plump rooster, all scarlet and black and gold, with his mane flared out and his wings half akimbo.

The tip of her tongue is held in her teeth, she lunges towards him and back, stooping down with her hands by her sides. He speaks, and she answers; little grunts come out of her throat; he scolds and she taunts him back.

He in his finery, treading the threshold. She in her yellow slicker, dancing.

Till the man comes down through the yard to rescue her, and the spell is broken. She sticks out her tongue — at which of them, looking back, it is hard to be sure — and darts inside the barn.

She comes out again with prison in her eyes.

"There are big girls in cages," she says.

It was not the milking stanchions, with their neck-iron manacles, nor the knee-deep layers of manure — it was the squalour, the swipes of shit along the walls higher than my eyes, the dust-bleared cobweb veils about every beam, with fat pallid spiders hanging in wait. The reek of despair.

Three crusted light bulbs. Eight cages slung from a beam. From each, with mad eyes, a hen stared back at us. Dry water bowls, seven eggs at the foot of each cage. The tenants had left a week before we turned up. Each bird with a clipped-off beak, roman nosed, insane.

What animals tell about people.

And the rooster, circling now in the doorway, blocked by our legs, uttering a weird, whining purl of frustration, why was he there? Not the gaoler, as he'd seemed, but a creature kept, like a teaser stallion or a sewn-up gomer bull, to set the girls' juices flowing.

We set them free. Twisting the wire catches loose, fetching water from the filthy milk parlour, waiting to see what would happen.

Casually, one at a time, they flapped down to the floor. No drought-truce for them: the dish of water was their measure of rank and favour. We might as well not have been there, their liberators. It wasn't nice; it was hard not to see it as human — some tyrant's court, some schoolyard manouevering, some revolutionary council. But they were quick — it was settled in less than a minute. And it endured.

The Queen Mother, the Duchess, the Countess, Milady — with her blotched finery of yellow and red against the others' brown dowds, with her only white eggs — and the four Mary's. But those names came little by little, in the week that followed. Oscar was first.

He could have been Rocky, or Egbert or Rufus or Punch, and when Aidan suggested Oscar during dinner that night — our first meal under the pressed-tin ceiling whose pattern so mesmerized Leni that she sat, mouth open, craning around like the little red hen — I said no, no, not a chance: let's keep Hollywood out of our world. But for Aidan there was a Fenian hero with more brawn than brain, from the far-off tales — Oscar Wilde was named for him, he told me, but I wasn't persuaded.

But later that night, when I'd scoured the bathtub within an inch of its life, and Leni lay half afloat there, in our well water, rocking and singing, the christening took place.

She leaned back, giggling, against my arm as I stroked the soap across her shoulders. Her six-year-old self, unafraid of anything. "Funny girl," I said. "What is it?" She just crowed with merriment — "Oscar," she said, "Oscar," and kicked her feet in a spasm of laughter so that the waves broke over her and ran up my arms — "Oscar, *Oss-curr!*" and I knew there would always be this ghost from now on, in the house. A girl upstairs, laughing, and the lapping of water. So he had his name.

He'd yet to come into his glory, though. His blustering, crestfallen, stubborn and comical glory.

Aidan lay fretting all night. He got up twice before dawn to go out to the barn. The weasels were closing in, the skunks and racoons from the swamps and the hedge-bottoms, drawn by our yard light, whetting their fangs for the necks of those dreaming chickens. The van was still half-unloaded, and had to be returned by the end of the day, but he was off before breakfast. Leni and I were eating on an upended trunk, surrounded by cartons and half-unpacked boxes when he came back down the driveway, with rolls of chicken wire poking like cannons from the car windows. "He's a big kid," I said. I was furious, actually. I wasn't unpacking that van on my own and he'd vanished into the barn. We went upstairs to get Leni's bedroom organized and a couple of hours later we were summoned to join in the roundup.

He'd converted the low horse stall at the end of the barn to a coop. Wire up to the rafters, nestboxes, feeders, water-bowls, perches. A big coolie-hat light hanging down. I forgave him — I don't know how he'd thought of it all, and it was so clumsily done, but it let me inside his mind. I wanted to ruffle his hair. We herded the chickens back into jail, while Oscar skulked round in the shadows, muttering and scolding. He wouldn't go in.

"Just for a night and a day," Aidan said. "Once they've laid some eggs they'll know it's home and come back every night." He was right about that, though I know he was only guessing.

Poor Oscar, though — whatever joy he'd had of the girls that first afternoon, he was shut out again.

And Miss Leni went hooting all afternoon, up the stairs, down the hall, in her room, wherever we turned. She meant us to hear her, the imp. She'd mimicked our lovemaking once, just after we got together: the moans and gasps, the ridiculous laugh I break into. They want you to know what they know, but don't want to be told. But this high, crooning warble that thrust out her lips as she smirked around the house, it was something else. Besides, we hadn't made love in a week. "What *is* this?"I said. It was getting on my nerves, and Aidan was no help — he was somehow enjoying it. "It's Oscar, Mom," she said. "Ask Aidan, he'll tell you." The first time, I think, they'd ever ganged up on me. "He's in love," Aidan said. "Go and see."

It was my turn. I went out in the dusk. We all found some private space in that barn, by and by.

He was lying on his side by the coop — really on his side, one wing under him, a yard from the makeshift door. His beak was agape and that pleading cry — of longing, of promise — filled up the barn. It just wouldn't stop. I felt it inside my ribs but the hens weren't impressed. They'd been hearing it all day, I imagine; maybe they'd heard that song all their time in those cages. One by one, as I watched, they hopped up on their perches, in strict pecking order, the Queen Mother first, and settled down. They were making drowsy clucks and murmurs when I left, and he was still serenading. I went back and turned off the light.

It was a week or more before I saw him romancing — "treading the hen" as they call it — and I quite see why. He was out by the fence, for the hens had their freedom now, wandering free through the days, all over the yard, even out in the pasture.

One moment he was feeding beside one of the Mary's. Next thing, her neck was gripped, pinched tight in his beak and he was up on her. His feet planted on her back, if you please, toes splayed on her stiff feathers. Her legs buckled, taking the weight of two. There they were, rumps in the air, her head almost on the floor. It made me shudder, to be truthful. I saw a couple, their startled faces together against the pillow, staring into the same nothing. Our faces.

Had she given some signal, had he? It was so sudden and silent and then, in the moment, so inert. And afterwards just a casual settling of feathers and tail, *frrrrt*, like a brolly-shake — then strangers, back to the grain and the grit and the casual bugs and crickets which Aidan said gave our eggs their dark, rich yolks. When he said that I went off eggs for a week. Some things are too damn organic up close.

Never mind that, it was our happiest time. Aidan was back at work, I'd the house to myself, and each day after school Leni collected eggs in the basket he'd bought for her. I'd supper ready when Aidan got home and then we'd be out, rain or shine, exploring, giving names to things, learning. And we fell into the ritual before bedtime of sitting on the long couch, sharing stories. The swallows left, but the Fall showed no sign of ending.

And Aidan wanted more animals. Maybe he'd run out of things to name, for that was his passion. The barn cats had names now, Court and Spark, and some of our land-marks too — we'd a Hanging Tree and a Moon Pond, and the knoll at the pasture's edge, where old lilacs groped among the cedars and the fireflies would wink at us come the Spring, was our Fairy Fort, for the one we once camped on in Donegal on our way to meet Aidan's grandmother.

But it was more than that, wasn't it — a foreknowledge or boding in him that needed to set things a-growing. He said to me once, after the tests came back, "You haven't just got Leni, there's your work. People will still be reading your words after you're dead." It was meant as a consolation. "I'll hear *your* voice," I said, "when you're dead." And I do.

There'd be sheep in the Spring, and a goat, and our neighbours' calves in the back stalls of the barn, but it started with game hens. The notion we'd get some meat in the freezer before Winter.

There was a flock of them by a house outside Holyrood — always out on the road, though we never saw one run over. I got talking one day in Miller's store to Joanne, who owned that place. "They're good for nothing," she told me. "They go broody at the drop of a hat, and hide their eggs out in the hedges. Next thing there's a dozen more of them under your feet." We were welcome, she said, to any we could catch, and she shook her head.

We drove down and stalked them that evening, snatching them off their perches in her garage, and into feed sacks. Five hens, one of them white, and a black rooster. We put them into the old driving shed with the cracked plexiglass skylight.

When we looked in before bedtime, they'd got up into the roof-trusses, the rooster highest of all. With the yard light through the dim plexiglass you could imagine their ancestors, dreaming on vine-draped branches, silhouettes in the jungle sky. These ones would never get names. They were like pheasants or partridges — wild things, with their intricate leafmeal plumage — how could we tell them apart? Except for the white one, and Leni at once chose a name for it. Lucy. Aidan rolled his eyes, and held his tongue. What would he have called it — Deirdre of the Sorrows? He'd a name himself ready, anyway, for the little black rooster — Raffles. It suited, I have to say: something raffish in his upright strut, his lean, gleaming neck, the bright, arrogant eyes.

We heard him crowing that night, as he would every night — a three-note article, quite different from Oscar's storybook cockalorums. And Oscar crowed only at dawn, or when one of the dames laid her egg.

The newcomers stayed in their shed for three days. Then came the bloodshed.

I didn't even know Aidan had stayed home that day. I'd a room cleared upstairs by then, with windows to south and west, fresh white walls and my desk at the centre. I'd a deadline too, but the work all seemed alien now. I was forcing myself, and the windows didn't help.

I was standing, looking down at the yard, watching Oscar actually, sunning himself on a gravel heap while the hens foraged about. In that light every colour and sheen of his feathers was on show. He was the fire bird.

Then Aidan came out of the barn and across to the driving shed. Did he know what was going to happen when he opened the door? Or guess at least?

Oscar stiffened, stepped down from the gravel heap and prepared for battle. He lowered his head and began to swell — from his mane back through his shoulders until he had doubled his size. He was huge now, fearsome — a mikado, a samurai, magnificent in the sunlight, waiting. Whereas Raffles, the closer he came, seemed almost to shrink into himself. He held his neck very erect, and it swayed a bit as he moved, a deliberate stalking past Aidan's legs and across the yard. He kept coming, and Oscar waited.

Something whispered in me what was going to happen. The little gamecock knew what he was about, and Oscar didn't. Raffles kept coming, and he was so small that he walked right under Oscar's chin. But as he passed he reached up and gave swift little pecks to both sides of Oscar's face. Then he strutted back out in a tight circle, and started again. Again and again. That's all he did — walk up, and under, and jab, jab, jab. Oscar didn't shift. He seemed to be waiting for the real fight to begin, by the real rules, and meanwhile the little upstart was putting his eyes out. This wasn't David and Goliath; it was torture.

Aidan just stood there. He was such a gentle person, he followed his thoughts through, about everything, till they curved back to confirm his feelings. When he daydreamed, his eyes were a young boy's. But who was he now, standing rigid with fascination? I could see the look on his face without having to see it, and it was sick. And why didn't I call down, put a stop to it myself?

The little assassin kept circling and coming back — and then Oscar simply deflated. His wings dragged on the earth, and he shuffled off, defeat, as they say, written all over him. All Raffles did then was let out a perfunctory crow, and start pecking around in the dirt as if nothing had happened.

Oscar was almost blinded, I think. He dragged himself off and Aidan was standing right in front of him. And the bird — I could tell — was so beaten that he could go no lower. He checked for a moment and then kept stubbornly coming; he didn't care; this human, so huge in front of him, was not going to stop him. A kind of courage below courage

— it broke my heart. And suddenly Aidan knelt down and held him, cradled him with the horrible, swollen face bleeding upon his shoulder, and carried him down to the barn.

Oscar moped in a corner behind the stanchions. And each day after school, Leni went down and squatted there, talking to him privately, in a stern big-sisterly way, as she might to one of her stuffed toys. Four days of that. At last Aidan said he would put him out of his misery. "It will break her heart," I said. He started to speak, but then looked away. "I know," I said. "She has to learn." He was trying. She wasn't his but he was trying.

And she knew more than us. Next morning Oscar was out in the yard, with his harem in tow. We waited for trouble and there was none. He and Raffles ignored each other. He took his hens out in the field, and paraded around, and came back in the yard and from then on he and Raffles would pass within feet of each other and have no reaction at all. They were all roosting in the stable coop now, on separate perches, as if they were different species. It didn't make sense.

No, the heartbreak didn't come with Oscar. It was Lucy. We found her clamped upon thirteen eggs up in the haymow, and next morning her body lay headless outside the barn. "Owls," said our neighbour, Bill Percy: "They rip off the heads and drink the blood, and that's all." Was it true? "You got livestock, you got dead stock," Bill laughed. Leni mourned, and I couldn't shake off the feeling that somehow our finding of Lucy's nest had led the killer to her. "That's weird," Aidan said, "it's exactly what I've been thinking."

Don't call coming "the little death"; the little deaths are the disappointments we see in our children' eyes as the world closes in and heaven slips further behind them.

Leni hated Raffles. She'd take on an awkward, teenagerish walk when she met him, and turn her face away. As if he cared. There was something functional about him, a lack of personality — the indifferent way he fed, and trod and stalked about in his own aura. Raffles was a psychopath I decided. Whereas Oscar — Oscar was a swaggering fellow who would weep in his beer. His emotions were all on the surface. His eye was a bankrupt nobleman's. He was a sensualist, a sentimentalist. Raffles never swaggered — he didn't care what anyone else thought. His eye was expressionless as the eye of a penis.

But Oscar was the breeder. One of the game hens turned up with nine chicks and as they grew we could tell who the father was. They were all roosters — *Bring forth men children only* — and black like Raffles, but they'd gay colours at head and tail and they were big. Aidan made them a pen and fed them on grain. The meat birds he called them.

And on top of that, it was Oscar the Hero now. We'd all been there when the brown goshawk came round the barnside and swooped on Milady. As it struggled to lift her, Oscar came charging to the rescue. It may have looked comical, Disneylike, with his waddling gallop and his silly face gaping as he let out that yodelling cry, but it felt ferocious. He hurled himself three feet into the air, clawing at the marauder, and the hawk dropped its prey and made off. We cheered and cheered. Oscar looked somewhat astonished with himself. And Milady was fine, though one wing drooped ever after.

Leni turned seven in October. Aidan stayed home all that day, busy with something up on the roof. To clean the chimney, you had to climb through the attic and onto a little platform, a yard square maybe, with a low parapet. That's where he was, hammering at something, full of his secret. When she unwrapped her gifts after school, there was a weathervane rooster, large as life. She loved it. "It's Oscar," she said. "Well it's like him alright," Aidan said, "but they can't have the same name." "He's Other Oscar," she told him.

I went out in the yard with the camera and watched them come out, her hand in his at that perilous height, and settle the weathercock on the rod Aidan had fixed there. Leni cheered and waved, and the iron bird swung in the breeze that blew hair across her face. It's all you can see in the photo. Other Oscar had a voice too — there was always a faint screech of metal on metal when the wind got up. And it did.

Our long benevolent Fall was gone in a night. Everything had unnatural sharp edges and the smokey blue haze on the face of the woodlots had vanished. Storm windows were on my mind. The leaves fled away in two days of west winds. Instead of small skyways through the foliage, like the white maze-trails on a printed page, the trees on the woodlot were skeletons, traceries, their garments put by.

There's a young man sitting at the edge of a light shaft, in an old dominie's chair. This is where he comes to be most himself. He can sit for an hour without stirring, watching the hens.

The sound of the birds, the ones that talk to themselves like old women, the ones that make dreamy duets, the flirts of their wings, the croon from a nest box and the gabble as an egg thuds on the straw, the scritch of their claws on the barn floor, the communal murmur as they drift on their perches towards silence.

The dust motes float in the light from the haymow.

I want him to be old; I want the thin cheekbones to be loosened and pouched by time; I want the hands that rest on each knee to be drawn and mottled by age; I want him to be a ghost in the future like that, long after our time has passed. But he is young, he will always be young. He is not thinking; he is wholly absorbed in watching. The roosters stand at each doorway, the daylight behind them, watching him in turn.

He will always be young, the cockbirds will outlive him.

It's his chair I am sitting in now, the chair that I wear as I write.

The neighbours' combines ran all night in the cornfields. Lights scanning our bedroom walls, the rumble of engines. There were geese on the pasture each day, and frost on our windshield. We wore hats and gloves when we went out on the land, discovering things that the season was laying bare.

For all of his naming it wasn't Aidan's way to talk about things that he loved. He touched them. As he touched me. Down by the drainage ditch, with his hand on the bark of the solitary yellow birch, he looked up at the woodlot and said, "No one should ever lay claim to more trees than he knows in person." I ducked under his arm and held him as if for the last time.

There's a young girl with sleep and bewilderment in her eyes standing at her mother's bedside. "The Oscars are shouting at each other," she whispers.

"It's just a dream," says the man who lies next to her mother. He reaches out for her: "Come on, climb in and get warm."

"No, listen," she says.

There are owls crying, loud and close in the cold night.

They get dressed and go outside. There's one owl on the barn, another up on the house roof. When they go out by the fence they can see that it's perched on the weathervane. The cries fill the night, and the sky behind is a tent of colours. Three little people, hand in hand, standing under the polar lights, while the owls speak, and dimly from inside the barn a three-note call defies them.

The haymow was dark now. We'd nailed up the hatches and dragged bales across the whole floor for insulation. Soon we'd be closing the barn up, too — the birds were all stay-at-homes now, the yolks of their eggs got paler every day.

The well pump was in the barn. We were making a shelter for it, against the cold, when I stumbled against the meatbirds' cage and their half-door flew open.

It happened too fast for belief. As if they'd been poised in wait.

The walls of the city were broken, the licentious soldiery stared down across the rubble, eyeing their spoils.

They hurled themselves onto the hens, pinning them down, treading one, then another, tearing feathers from their necks, a pandemonium of lust.

I went after them with a broom, but Aidan grabbed my arm. "Let them get it over with," he said, and grinned into my face: "*A hard cock hath no conscience.*"

"Jesus," I said, wrestling myself loose.

"No, Saint Augustine."

I hated him — I ran among the rapists, scattering them. I'd have killed each one of them if I could. I went back to the house and didn't see him till nightfall.

Leni came in with the eggs, pouting. "Aidan's killing the meatbirds," she said. "He won't let me watch." "I should think not," I said, but I was tracing his thoughts. "Why would you want to watch that — headless chickens chasing you round? Blood everywhere."

"He said they don't run if you mark a cross on the chopping block first."

She stood at the mudroom window, imagining, as I was. He came and went at the milk parlour door, and we could hear the axe. In my mind the great shadow of his arm was rising and falling on the barn wall.

I heard him below at the basement door, and the freezer open and close. He came in and went straight up to the bathroom. The shower ran till it went cold.

"I'll sleep on the couch," he said, "I can't get the stink off me. I can taste it. It's in everything."

I went down and joined him in the night.

The first day of snow I discovered the Queen Mother's secret. She'd had a nest, and there on the muddy floor of the driving shed, in the tiniest ray of sunshine, was the one surviving chick, shivering, bare. If I'd thought it would survive I'd have brought it into the house, but I turned away.

It did survive, though. As though she knew, she got it into the barn the day we closed all the doors. It fed, and it grew, but it was naked. Except for the wings and a straggly ruff about its neck, the feathers never came. I don't know how it stayed alive. And each night the temperature fell.

Late November, snow drifting along the fenceline, ice locking the windows. I went down to the barn to bring in the water bowls and get any late eggs before they could freeze. The cold inside a barn is like no other cold; it seems to come from inside — there, out of the real weather — it's still, and hollow, and full of suspended odours. The stable was a room of light at the heart of it. I sat in Aidan's chair and watched the sleeping birds. The chill began to creep into me. The house seemed a world away, with its warmth and smells and Aidan reading to Leni on the couch. As if the chickens and I could disappear into an ice age and never be found.

I made myself get up and go into the coop. No eggs. The water bowls frozen solid, of course. The chickens' faces level with mine.

And I realized the naked chick was not there. A rat might have got it, but then there'd be a carcass — there was no hole to drag the body out through. I looked at those dreaming faces again — cannibals? It was a wonder, really, they hadn't picked on the little cripple before. Then I saw Raffles' broken wing — hanging down on the perch like Milady's. Something must have got into the coop — a mink, a skunk? — and been scared off by me. I would have to get Aidan down and check for gaps in the wire before they were all slaughtered.

But it wasn't a broken wing, it was shelter. Two other feet were perched beside Raffles'. He was holding the naked chick against him, sharing his warmth.

I could see myself, tiptoeing out, with a backward look like a servant girl in an old painting, wide-eyed at some miracle.

Outside, the snow was tumbling about the yard light, flailed by the wind. I could hear Other Oscar faintly behind it, and my own boots squeaking upon the snow. Well, these were the first tears I'd shed in our four months here. There were more to come — more tears in the year ahead than I thought there could be in the world — but as I walked towards the house, looking up at the lights where the story was being told, I knew that a woman weeping in the snow would haunt this place for ever.

But would anyone who saw her, or heard of her, and was told the story of our lives, ever guess at the small and sufficient reason for her tears?

THE BUSH ON THE GRAVE

LLOYD RATZLAFF

IN THE PIONEER CEMETERY beside Diefenbaker Park near my home in Saskatoon, there is a grave on which a chokecherry bush is growing, hanging heavily some autumns with ripe black fruit. Vandals often desecrate other graves in that place, but as far as I know, they've never damaged this one. Beside the South Saskatchewan River, in the middle of a patch of prairie, in the centre of a grave, the bush stands over the remains of a little boy named Vernon Leo Kuhn, who lived in this world for six months in 1902 and 1903. It's the only bush of its kind in the cemetery. I have often thought that, if it were done respectfully, those dangling clusters of cherries could be made into a unique wine. But no one ever seems to pick them; perhaps people are too superstitious to do it, or perhaps some fluke of nature allows them to ripen there until a person such as I comes along, ripe himself for the kind of experience which befell me there one afternoon of the first of September.

I don't say I would have felt free to pick those chokecherries if I had intended simply to make a drinking wine. For wine and its related spirits have sometimes caused me more trouble than they were worth. But when I set out for the cemetery with a plastic pail in the late afternoon sun, I pondered the untidy leave I had taken of my family's Christian fundamentalism — affirming the leave-taking, but regretting the pain — and hoped for a sacramental wine to come of my day's endeavour.

I passed through a clump of poplars bordering the cemetery, where a magpie jabbered at it knew what, and stepped onto prairie grass toward the little plot where a century ago an infant was lowered into the earth by its grieving relatives, and shovelled over, and left to the straying forms of life which would overtake that parcel of ground. Winds would blow, animals would forage, seeds would fall, and one of them would strike roots toward the child. One day the navel of the earth would open, and a plant would come up and turn into this bush, which so many years later had produced the cherries before which I stood with my pail.

The chokecherries will become wine, will become me — Vernon Leo Kuhn will become me. So arrested was I by this thought, that I sat down before the weathered tombstone to commune with the child. My tradition's sense of the sacramental had been so sparse, its means of grace so subjective and elusive.

"I don't know," I said to Vernon Leo, "how it is that you were here for such a short time; but I want to tell you that a tree has come from your body. There was a seed which found you with its roots, and the roots took you up into the air, into a bush, with some help from the light and wind and water from the sky. And the cherries on it, little boy, are wonderfully sweet; I know that, because the other day I tasted them, and now I'm going to pick them to make some wine."

Here I was required to make a promise; the choke in the cherries wasn't lost on me. "I've done some foolish things,"

I said, "with some other wines, but this one will be different. This is your lifeblood, and I wish it to become mine."

A gate opened. I saw all things existing by virtue of consuming and being consumed; I saw that this is how things are, and how the world is therefore the body of God. In the autumnal light I got up to pick chokecherries, and they rolled from the branches through my fingers, funnelling through cupped hands into the pail hanging at my belt. For once, my hands, not my head, did the picking. When my head picks chokecherries, branches are broken, leaves are torn, fruit is squashed; this time my hands knew what to do, though my mind reminded me that later I would crush those cherries to a bloody pulp and trample them like Yahweh in his winepress.

"I Am," I said to the bush, uncertainly at first, then more boldly, "I am the I AM-ness." And with that, I had broken through the sometimes-despairing, sometimes-defiant sound of it, to the name of God: I AM what I am — that is my name for all time, by which I shall be invoked for all generations to come. The Jewish text and the Christian eucharist echoed a Zen monk's joy: "I eat food, I am food!"

My death ceased to matter. I was able to say I AM and not require that it refer to myself, or not only to myself. Or it did matter — to creatures who fly and burrow and creep and swim, or who stand growing in one spot, who surrender their lives when I eat them; who, when the translation of all languages is done, also say I AM, as I do. For an hour I picked chokecherries, while the world was one round mellowness within and around, and tenderness and clarity and trust. I was Caleb, weighted with vintage from the promised land; or I was John Donne in heaven, where it is always autumn, for things are ever at their maturity.

The mystics have always been confident that we don't have to go anywhere, for I AM is where we are — at this bush with the baby and the cherries, in the city with its impetuous horns and lonely terrors. Vernon Leo Kuhn never imagined himself as a human ego with a name, never emerged far enough to confuse himself with some lost and disconnected thing which only we — and we falsely — had supposed him to be. We are lower-case i's; but Vernon Leo stayed nearly enough I AM for that pestiferous ego never to have taken shape, and he of the scarcely-sexual body didn't have to travel nearly so far back as the rest of us.

Mother Julian of Norwich said, "I was shown no hell harder than sin." We puzzle and fret and fight over our straying from the communion we once knew; and sin becomes a strange word as it becomes a familiar experience. And repentance, that other strange word, means: How could I have forgotten? Thank God, now I remember.

A dead child under a chokecherry bush. Sweet wine.

BIOGRAPHICAL NOTES

BRIAN BRETT was born in Vancouver, and spent his childhood on the road in his father's truck, learning the Fraser Valley farm region, the native villages, and ocean and lakeside fishing camps. He ruined his knees walking over too many mountains, and has had too many opportunities to witness the destruction of the great raincoast cloud forest and the rich delta of the Fraser River. A poet, novelist, and journalist, the author of ten books, his latest publication is *The Colour of Bones in a Stream* (Sono Nis Press 1998). His natural habitat is limited to the climate region where the wild rhododendron grows. He has spent his adult life advocating the preservation of this ecology. Currently, he lives on an organic farm on Saltspring Island, British Columbia.

Novelist and poet BARRY CALLAGHAN is included in every major Canadian anthology and his fiction and poetry have been translated into seven languages. His works include *The Hogg Poems and Drawings* (General 1978), *The Black Queen Stories* (Lester & Orpen Dennys 1982), *The Way The Angel Spreads Her Wings* (Lester & Orpen Dennys 1989), *When Things Get Worst* (Little, Brown & Co. 1993), *A Kiss Is Still A Kiss* (Little, Brown & Co. 1995), *Hogg, The Poems And Drawings* (Carleton 1997), *Barrelhouse Kings: A Memoir* (Little, Brown & Co. 1998), and *Hogg: The Seven Last*

Words. He has published translations of French, Serbian, and Latvian poetry, and has been writer-in-residence at the universities of Rome, Venice, and Bologna. He was a war correspondent in the Middle East and Africa in the 1970s, and at the same time began the internationally celebrated quarterly and press, *Exile* and Exile Editions.

Ecologist and writer **DON GAYTON** is the author of two award-winning books of creative non-fiction, *The Wheatgrass Mechanism* (Fifth House 1990), and *Landscapes of the Interior* (New Society Publishers 1997). His work has appeared in numerous anthologies as well as in magazines such as *Canadian Geographic, Equinox* and *Harrowsmith.* Don has lived in the Canadian prairies, the Western US and South America, working variously as a cowboy, community development worker, agricultural extension agent and ecosystem management specialist. He lives with his family in Nelson, BC, and is currently working on a book about the grasslands of Canada.

TERRY GLAVIN is a British Columbian author, critic, journalist and conservationist. He left a career in daily newspapers in 1993 and has since written six books, co-authored two books, and his work for magazines such as *Canadian Geographic, Outdoors Canada,* and *The Georgia Straight* have earned him several National Magazine Awards and regional writing awards. His 1996 collection of essays *This Ragged Place* (New Star Books), was shortlisted for the Governor-General's Awards non-fiction prize. His most recent book, *The Last Great Sea: A Voyage Through the Human and Natural History of the North Pacific Ocean* (Greystone Books 2000), was the 2001 winner of the Hubert Evans Prize. He was also the recipient of the 2001 Roderick Haig-Brown conservation award issued by the International North Pacific Chapter of the American Fisheries Society. Terry Glavin lives in a heavily-armed compound on Mayne Island, in British Columbia's southern gulf islands.

PRUDENCE GRIEVE writes fiction under another name.

TREVOR HERRIOT is a prairie naturalist and writer who lives on an old glacial lakebed that has recently seen its native wheat grass, buffalo, and burrowing owls replaced by wheat farms, gravel roads and a city of 200,000 people who live in buildings with foundations that lurch and crack with every shift of the Pleistocene gumbo. His first book, *River in a Dry Land: a Prairie Passage* (Stoddart 2000), blends personal memoir with natural history, family legend and social commentary to shed light upon the cultural and ecological tragedies of a single watershed in the Northern Great Plains. It was shortlisted for the 2000 Governor General's Award for Non-fiction, won Book of the Year at the 2000 Saskatchewan Book Awards, the 2000 Drainie-Taylor Biography Prize (Writers Trust of Canada), and the 2000 Canadian Booksellers Association Libris Award for First-Time Author of the Year. Herriot goes regularly with his wife and four children to a cabin in Saskatchewan's Qu'Appelle Valley where, between birdwatching, beekeeping, and fixing the roof, he can usually find ways to put off working on his next book.

PATRICK LANE was born in and has lived much of his life in British Columbia and considers himself a natural naturalist, someone who has wandered with an inquiring body and mind from southern Chile to the far north of Canada, and always with an abiding love for the great wilderness where he grew up, the Kootenay and Okanagan valleys of the West. His latest collections of poetry are, *The Bare Plum of Winter Rain* and *Selected*

Poems 1977-1997, both published by Harbour Publishing. In 2003 he will publish *What We Are Is A Garden*, a twelve-month meditation on gardening. He is presently completing a new collection of poetry and is compiling a book of his short fiction, both new and old. The author of twenty-eight books, he has received most of the literary awards in Canada and, as well, has travelled the world, reading from his work. His poems have been translated into sixteen languages. An earlier version of "The Snake-Grass Hills" appeared in *Geist* magazine.

STEVEN LATTEY was born and raised in the Okanagan Valley, which has been the setting for many of his stories. "The stories, up until now, have always been a blend of fact and fiction. In doing this I hoped to entertain, to get closer to some naked truth and to make some money. Two out of three would be fine. The Okanagan story in this book is my first attempt at, 'death defying journalism'. I hope it's my last. Because of the subject matter, I have tried to stick to the facts as I saw them and record an extraordinary event." Steven Lattey is the author of the short fiction collection *Aphid & the Shadow Drinkers* (Thistledown 1999).

TIM LILBURN is the author of the poetry collections *To the River* (McLelland & Stewart 1999), *Living in the World as if It Were Home* (Cormorant Books 1999), and *Moosewood Sandhills* (McLelland & Stewart 1994). He also is the editor of *Poetry and Knowing* (Quarry 1995) and *Thinking and Singing: Poetry and the Practice of Philosophy* (Cormorant 2002), essay collections on poetics. He teaches philosophy and literature at St. Peter's College, Muenster, Saskatchewan. "Getting into the Cabri Lake Area" has also appeared in *BRICK*, a literary journal.

DON MCKAY's most recent book, *Vis a Vis: field notes on poetry and wilderness* (Gaspereau 2001) includes thoughts on both the poetics and politics of nature poetry. He is the author of nine books of poetry, including two which won the Governor General's Award: *Night Field* (McClelland & Stewart 1991) and *Another Gravity* (McClelland & Stewart 2000). All of McKay's creative work is inspired by encounters with the natural world in general, and birds in particular. He lives in Victoria, British Columbia.

DAVIDA MONK is a performer, choreographer, teacher and writer. She began her dance career with Le Groupe de la Place Royale of Ottawa. In addition to dancing and making work for the company, she served as Assistant Artistic Director to Artistic Director Peter Boneham and helped to develop Canada's only choreographic dance lab. Her works have been seen across Canada and in Poland and Finland. She has danced the works of more than twenty choreographers. Her written work has focused primarily on her experiences in dance. Her interest in landscape writing dates from her first visit to the Saskatchewan prairies in 1985. A love of the Cypress Hills brought her to Alberta, where she has made her home since 1992. Dancing in the natural prairie is a regular part of her practice. Davida Monk is on faculty at the Program of Dance, University of Calgary, Alberta.

SUSAN MUSGRAVE is a poet, novelist, children's writer, essayist, and columnist. She lives on Vancouver Island, and, whenever she can get away, on the Queen Charlotte Islands/Haida Gwaii. Her most recent books are the novel *Cargo of Orchids* (Knopf 2000), *What the Small Day Cannot Hold: Collected Poems 1970-1985* (Beach Holme 2000) and *Things That Keep and Do Not Change* (McClelland & Stewart 1999). She has been nominated, and has received awards, in five different categories of writing: poetry, fiction, non-fiction, personal essay, children's writing and for her work as an editor. In 1996 she received the Tilden (CBC/Saturday Night) Canadian Literary Award for Poetry, and the Vicky Metcalf Short Story Editor's Award.

ILLTYD PERKINS came to Canada thirty-four years ago, lasted a couple of years in the English Department at the University of Victoria, and since then has worked building boats, furniture, and a house. He lives on Saltspring Island.

LLOYD RATZLAFF is a prairie writer whose literary and academic work has appeared in several dozen North American magazines and journals. He is a former minister, counsellor, and university lecturer. His first book *The Crow Who Tampered With Time* — a collection of essays grounded in the Saskatchewan landscape — was published in the spring of 2002 by Thistledown Press. He lives in Saskatoon, Saskatchewan. Earlier versions of "The Bush on the Grave" appeared in *Quest Magazine* and *Prairie Messenger*.

In the early years of the twentieth century, the Government of Canada granted some of JAN ZWICKY's ancestors a homestead on SW32-57-08-W5, a quarter section of scrub parkland in the home territory of the Cree at the extreme northwest edge of the Great Plains. It is a place she herself still calls home, although the political and philosophical implications of so doing appear increasingly complex. She is the author of a number of books of poetry and philosophy, including *Songs for Relinquishing the Earth* (Brick 1998) for which she received the Governor General's Award, and *Lyric Philosophy* (University of Toronto Press 1992). Her latest book *Wisdom and Metaphor* is forthcoming from Gaspereau Press in 2003. She currently lives in Victoria, British Columbia.

AGMV Marquis

MEMBER OF SCABRINI MEDIA

Quebec, Canada
2002